PRAISE FOR BEATRICE BOWLES

"World stories are a treasure of humankind. I love the stories Beatrice brings to us!"
—Jack Kornfield, Spirit Rock Center, Teacher, Writer: A Path with Heart

"Wow! Not only are you a brilliant storyteller, but your pleasure in telling the tales deepens the power of the performance. My crew and I listened, enthralled."
—Helen Whitney, PBS filmmaker, NY, NY

"Amita listens to 'Heaven's A Garden in the Heart' every morning on the way to school. She already knows 'Monkey King' and 'The Perilous Pomegranate' by heart!"
—John Krich, Writer, Wall Street Journal, Planet Shanghai

"You are the best storyteller I have ever heard."
—Lucia, Age 6, Sunnybrae Elementary School, San Mateo, CA

"Beatrice's spirited myths and stories give children a true understanding of Nature's sacredness in all nations and foster their own 'green wisdom.'"
—Bob Hyland, Vice President, Brooklyn Botanical Gardens, Brooklyn, NY

"Oh, Monkey King is so wonderfully told with such lively imagination! The story is great fun for kids because they relate to Monkey King who is always restless, jumpy, and bored!"
—Eric Wu, Teen Leader, Chinatown Alleyway Tours, San Francisco, CA

"Your stories are suspenseful, mind-boggling, mysterious, exciting, funny, mystical, happy, and off the wall!"
—David, Age 9, Bank Street School, New York City, NY

"What an engaging retelling of stories, shimmering with the magic of creation!"
—Malcolm Margolin, Publisher, Heyday Books, Berkeley, CA

Spider Grandmother's Web of Wonders

Beatrice Bowles

Spider Grandmother's Web of Wonders

ISBN (hardcover edition): 978-0-9857901-1-0

ISBN (e-book edition): 978-0-9857901-3-4

ISBN (audio edition): 978-0-9857901-0-3

Published by Harmony Hill Productions.

San Francisco, California, U.S.A.

To contact the author, please visit www.beatricebowles.com.

Requests for appearances by the author are welcome, as are requests for educational and library pricing.

Design by Ashley Ingram (www.ashleyingramdesign.com)

Photo of Beatrice Bowles by Nancy Dionne (www.nancydionne.com)

Floral photos by Ted P. Kipping (treeshapers.com)

This book consists of stories for children based on traditional tales. For sources of the stories, please go to Beatrice Bowles's website at www.beatricebowles.com.

If I had influence with the good fairy who is supposed to preside
over the christening of all children,
I should ask that her gift to each child in the world be a sense of wonder
so indestructible that it would last throughout life....

Rachel Carson, *The Sense of Wonder*

CONTENTS

How Did Life Begin?

Jose Rey Toledo, the Hopi-Tewa artist who gave me permission to tell this story, said, "Teach children to listen for Spider Grandmother's little voice, for she still whispers wisdom to guide us, if we learn to listen."

On the island of Bali, in Indonesia, a woodcarver I met told this story about a creator who uses his own body to make the world.

The Makiritare people, who have lived along the Orinoco River for thousands of years, worship a sky god, Wanadi, who creates copies of himself to send to Earth.

In the Finnish national epic *The Kalevala,* bits of ancient poems and songs have been stitched together into this story of creation centered on the relationship between a mother goddess and her rebellious daughter.

How Is Everything Connected?

Why Are We Here?

INTRODUCTION

How did life begin?
How is everything connected?
Why are we here?

As a child, I found intriguing answers to those questions in my grandmother's beautiful storybooks. Myths from many lands told how miraculous forces had created Earth and Sky.

Fairy tales showed how kindness to others and to nature mattered and could bring surprising rewards. Folktales about young people or little creatures who outwitted bullies gave me courage, hope, and faith in justice. I read the stories over and over, as if my life depended on them.

Years later, when I read those same stories to my own children, I felt like a gardener planting magic seeds. My daughter and son's delight in hearing these stories inspired me to become a storyteller. Becoming a storyteller seemed like a call to adventure, and a crafty way to connect modern audiences with knowledge that often gets ignored or left behind.

In 1988, I attended my first conference on storytelling in Santa Fe, New Mexico. On the first night, I stood outside under the stars, wondering about my role as a storyteller. From the dark, a voice whispered, "Teach children to wonder." Startled, I hurried inside.

On stage, Jose Rey Toledo, a tall Hopi-Tewa artist with long white braids, was telling a story about how Spider Grandmother and Grandfather Sun sang up the world with a song. Then in three successive journeys led by Spider Grandmother, first insects appeared, then animals, and finally people. Because people could listen and learn, Spider Grandmother taught them to sing, dance, plant, weave, and give thanks for life on Earth. But in time, when evil leaders chanted, "Fight! Hate! Hoard! Gamble!," many people listened and ruined the third world. Only a faithful few found their way to this, the fourth world, where we live now.

A tiny spider and the mighty sun as the grandparents of life? Two loving forces at the heart of creation? The story's healing vision of nature and of the challenges of human nature stunned me. Our challenge, the story implies, is to heed Spider Grandmother's warnings against the four evils of fighting, hating, hoarding, and gambling, and to care for each other and for our miraculous gift: the vast but fragile web of life on Earth. Jose Rey Toledo's story was not only a tale of sweeping grandeur but a warning against the same evils that bedevil life today, and perhaps more than ever.

After Jose Rey Toledo gave me permission to tell his story, he added, "Spider Grandmother still whispers wisdom to children about the risky road of life, so be sure you tell them to listen."

In this book, inspired by Spider Grandmother's craft, I have gathered twenty-five of my favorite stories from different cultures and written them down as I tell them to children. Just as flowers growing together in the wild or in a garden heighten each others' beauty, these powerful stories deepen each others' impact. To echo that concept, I asked my friend Ted P. Kipping, an arborist and artist, to add his luminous photographs to these pages. I hope these stories spark bold new imaginings about how to care for ourselves, our children, other creatures, and our magnificent planet. Discover the joy of reading the stories aloud, or even of learning to tell them by heart, and please share the wonder with a child or a friend.

Luckily, Spider Grandmother still lives on in each of us as the power of imagination. Her wise little voice is always there, ready to guide us on the risky road of life—if we remember to listen. Perhaps she will even startle you into seeing as spiders do, with many eyes instead of only two.

1. THE LONG, DANGEROUS JOURNEY
(Arizona)

Alone in endless emptiness, Spider Grandmother drifted on the dark winds of space, dreaming of wonders to come. In a burst of light, she awoke, and there was Grandfather Sun. Then he, the brightest light in the universe, and she, the dark little weaver of wonders, swayed to the music of their voices, sang the first song, and created the first world—a great ball of rock with a cave full of insects.

Spider Grandmother jumped with joy at the sight of all the little spiders. But Grandfather Sun was disappointed by the buzzing and chattering in the dark. Something seemed to be missing. So the two grandparents of life sat side by side and sang a new song and brought forth a second world.

Spider Grandmother went to the insects. "Follow me and don't wander off, or you might be left behind, lost forever in the dark."

The insects stumbled after her on the long, dangerous journey up to the second world, where there was more light. Spider Grandmother began to weave more wonders from her dreams: trees, flowers, rivers, mountains, birds, animals, and more spiders, too.

But again, Grandfather Sun felt that something was missing. Since he was certain and she was curious, they sang a third song and brought forth a third world.

Spider Grandmother went to the insects and animals. "Follow me and don't wander off, or you might be lost forever in the dark." On the long, dangerous journey up to the third world, where there was even more light, some of the animals turned into the first people.

At last, Grandfather Sun was pleased. People could listen, learn, dream, sing and dance, and give thanks for life on Earth. Spider Grandmother taught women to build houses, to grow and grind corn, and to make pottery. She taught men to build kivas—underground rooms for sacred dances—and to hunt and to weave.

At night, the people slept under Spider Grandmother's sparkling veil, and at sunrise, they welcomed Grandfather Sun.

At last, the creators agreed. Creation seemed complete.

But over time, some people forgot to give thanks for life on Earth. Then evil leaders appeared among the people and urged them to fight, hate, hoard, and gamble. People began to take whatever they could from each other and from nature. Children were left unclean, unloved, and untaught.

Spider Grandmother warned that they were ruining their lives, but the faithless people mocked her. "Why listen to a spider? Men should rule nature and women. Nature has no feelings, and women have too many."

Grandfather Sun's temper grew hotter and hotter as he watched the third world ruin its own happiness. Spider Grandmother told the few faithful people, "You must leave and find a new home." This time, she made no offer to lead the way. No one knew what to do.

A wise old man said, "Have we not heard footsteps in the sky? There must be another world up there."

A brave little catbird offered to fly up through a hole in the sky to explore. Soaring out over a vast, empty desert, she saw only one creature: a man sleeping with his head on his knees. The catbird alighted and sang.

The man lifted his head. His eyes were deep set and burning bright. Jagged black lines crisscrossed his cheeks. On his chest hung a necklace of bones and teeth. It was Death.

"Are you not afraid?" asked Death.

"Yes...yes...but no," said the catbird. "Our world is being destroyed. Will you share this world with us?"

Death stared out over the empty desert. "Come, then. Come if you want to." Death laughed so strangely.

The catbird raced down to the third world to report. The good people decided to share the new world with Death rather than stay and be destroyed. But without Spider Grandmother's help, how could they make the long, dangerous journey?

Chipmunk popped out of his underground home with a magic seed and planted it in the ground. "Now sing, sing to make it grow!"

People sang and the bamboo grew. Every time people paused for breath, Spider Grandmother danced around the bamboo stalk to give them courage. Those rings around bamboo stalks mark where the people paused for breath. You can still see them for yourself.

At sunset, the tip of the bamboo passed through the hole in the sky.

Soon, people were climbing up the stalk. As they arrived in the fourth world, Mockingbird assigned a tribe and a language to each one. That night, for the last time, the tribes camped together around the bamboo, happy, weary, and closer to the stars than ever before.

Just after midnight, terrible noises woke them. Evil leaders from below were climbing the bamboo, cursing and shouting.

The good people in the fourth world shook the bamboo stalk so hard that they pulled the roots out of the ground. With a thunderous crash, the great bamboo fell back into the third world, taking those evil leaders along. As the sun rose on the fourth world, the tribes set off to find their new homes.

Grandmother Spider and Grandfather Sun watched the fourth world, as they still do today, carefully and full of hope.

2. OUT OF A SPINNING SHELL
(Indonesia)

For a long time, Ta'aroa (for that is the creator's name) lived alone in a shell that spun in endless darkness. There was no sun, and no moon, no earth, no mountains, no man, no woman, no dog, no bird, and no fresh water. There was only Ta'aroa spinning in the shell.

At last, Ta'aroa grew bored and began to scratch on the shell. Suddenly the shell cracked in two, and Ta'aroa slipped out, stood upon the shell, and called, "Who is out there?"

No voice answered.

"O rock, come over here! O sand, come up here!" cried Ta'aroa.

But no sand appeared, and there was no rock anywhere.

Because his commands were not obeyed, Ta'aroa went to work. He lifted up the top half of his shell and made a dome for the sky. The lower half he made into rock and sand. Still Ta'aroa was not content, so he made his spine into a mountain range, his ribs into green hills, his liver and lungs into broad floating clouds, his flesh into the fatness of Earth, his fingernails and toenails into scales

for fishes and shells, his feathers into trees, and his intestines into lobsters, eels, and shrimp for the rivers and seas.

Because of all this work, Ta'aroa's blood grew so hot that it floated away to make redness for the sky, for sunrises and sunsets, and for rainbows. Ta'aroa remains undestroyed and lives on as creator of everything.

As Ta'aroa had a shell, so everything has a shell. The sky is a shell of space for the sun, the moon, and the stars. Earth is a shell for stones, sand, water, plants, and animals and fish. Man's shell is woman because through woman he comes into the world. Woman's shell is woman because she, too, comes through woman. We cannot ever count all the shells of all the things that this world creates.

3. THE HIDDEN BALL

(Venezuela)

In the beginning, good, kind people lived in the sky world, where death, sickness, evil, and war never came. No one had to work or to hunt. Food was everywhere. There were no demons, no clouds, no storms, no winds, and no animals. The sun shone all the time because the sky god, Wanadi, lit everything from the top of the sky down to Earth below. There was no door between Earth and sky as there is today. Sky people lived happily in their villages. No one lived on Earth.

Wanadi decided to create people for Earth. First, he sent down a copy of his own spirit. This spirit, Wanadi the Wise One, brought with him knowledge and songs. He made the first people. But trouble came quickly. When Wanadi the Wise One was born, he had cut and buried his own navel cord, but worms got into the navel cord and produced an ugly creature covered with hair, Odosha the Evil One. Odosha sprang out of the Earth like a spear. "Earth is mine!" he screamed. "I'm going to chase away Wanadi the Wise One. This is war!"

First Odosha tricked people. A man went fishing and caught lots of fish. Odosha whispered to his neighbors, "Kill the man and then you will have lots of fish." When people killed the man and took his fish, Odosha was happy.

Wanadi the Wise One was furious. As punishment, Wanadi turned the first people into animals. Then he moved back up to the sky world, leaving only Odosha and the animals on Earth.

After a time, Wanadi thought, "I still want good people to live on Earth," so he sent down a second copy of himself. This Wanadi brought something special with him, Huehanna, a great ball with a shell of stone. Inside Huehanna, good, kind, happy people sang and laughed and told stories.

One day, Wanadi the Wise One told his nephew Irakuru to guard Huehanna while he went hunting. Wanadi left behind the magic bag in which he kept his power and the night. In those days the sun shone all the time, so when Wanadi got tired, he put his head into the magic bag and slept. "Remember," he warned Irakuru, "do not open my magic bag."

But no sooner had Wanadi left than Irakuru felt curious about the magic bag. A voice nearby whispered, "Open the bag! Open the bag!" This was Odosha, of course.

Irakuru opened the bag.

All at once, the world went dark.

Irakuru ran around in terror, screaming like a white monkey, and that's just the way he stayed. All white monkeys today are called Irakuru because of that boy Irakuru who let out the night so long ago.

Odosha shrieked, "Now I rule Earth! Let Wanadi try to bring anyone to life in this darkness." Odosha had heard a rumor that Wanadi was about to bring his mother to life again. Suddenly, Odosha felt the Earth crack open.

Wanadi's mother began to rise from her grave.

Odosha squirted burning poison on her body and scorched her flesh and bones.

When Wanadi arrived at his mother's grave, he found only ashes and bones. He hurried to find

Huehanna. The people inside were screaming in fright because Odosha had been beating on the ball with his club. So Wanadi hid the ball high in the mountains. The good people inside still haven't been born and they haven't died. They are waiting for Odosha's death, when hate, greed, and war will disappear.

Wanadi the Wise One will know when the time has come for the good people to come out.

4. MOTHER AIR, MOTHER WATER

(Finland)

In the beginning, Mother Air floated alone above an empty ocean. At last, out of loneliness and longing, she gave birth to a daughter fine and fair. All through her childhood, the daughter of Air wandered through her mother's splendid castles in the clouds. But finally the girl grew restless, and her restlessness grew stronger than her love of home.

One day, without a word of farewell, the girl left and went down to live on the ocean below.

In grief and fury, Mother Air sent down a howling tempest. Waves blew wild and high, tossing the daughter of Air on the billows, but, being a strong swimmer, the girl survived. During the long storm, the girl became a woman known forever after as Mother Water.

The wind and the sea had awakened new life in Mother Water. For seven centuries, nine times longer than a lifetime, Mother Water swam pregnant and alone. North, south, east, and west she swam, yet no child was born.

"Oh, I wish I had stayed a child wandering in my mother's castles in clouds," she cried. "Why must I drift so long, so full and heavy on the waves! O Mother Air, please free me from my burden!"

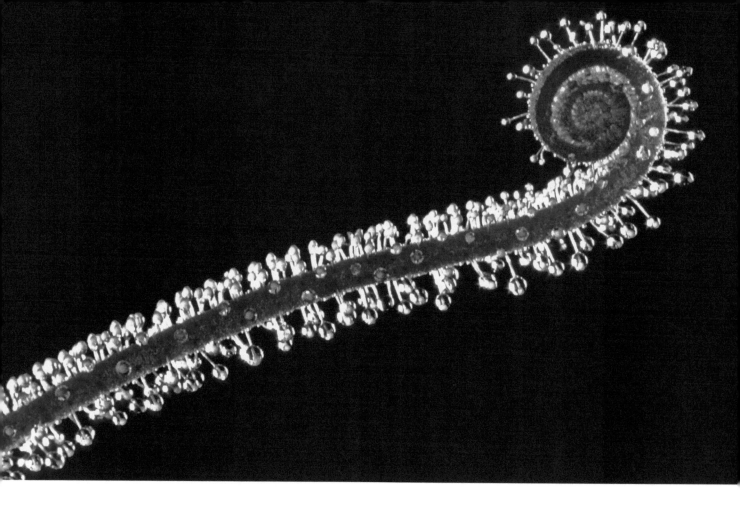

But still no child was born. When a wild duck flew over, searching for a home, Mother Water lifted her knees out of the sea so that the duck might have a place to rest. Thinking it was a green and flowered hill she saw, the duck landed, built a nest, and lay six gold eggs in it and a seventh of iron. For many days, the duck brooded on her nest.

Mother Water's knees grew warmer and warmer until they became burning hot. Her legs began to shake, and the eggs spilled into the ocean. But as they fell, a wondrous change came over them.

From the top half of one eggshell, up floated the great blue arch of sky. From a yolk, out spun the blazing sun. From an egg white, the glowing moon arose. Speckles in the whites became stars, and milky parts became clouds.

By the new lights, Mother Water lifted her hands and began to give order to creation. She formed the jutting headlands and the broad continents. Diving deep, she formed the ocean floor, carving caves for sheltering fishes. Then she sculpted bays and reefs and islands. She made mountains to hold up the sky. She signed rocks and hills with secret marks that we still can see, but only she can read.

Now Mother Water's child had rested in her belly for more than seven centuries. For thirty more summers and thirty more winters, the child thought and thought. Finally he spoke, "O Sun and Moon! Free me from this little nest. Let me see my mother's face. Let me feel the open air and see the sun and moon and stars above!" But the sun did not set him free, nor did the moon. The boy pounded against his mother's bones until he fell headlong into the sea, where his joyful mother caught him in her arms. For eight years more, mother and son drifted together on the waves until they came to a nameless, treeless, barren shore.

Mother Water's son stepped ashore. Finally he looked out over his mother's beautiful wide, blue face, and up at his grandmother's beaming face, and he watched the moon and stars by night. As the grandson of Mother Air and the son of Mother Water walked across the land, he gathered up seeds of every kind and scattered them about. Trees and plants sprouted up, and the barren Earth became a garden for all living things.

5. ICE HEART AND THE BEAMING MAIDEN (Alaska)

Long ago, when Raven, the wide-winged bird of night, was god, there was no sun, no moon, and no stars in the sky, only dark, endless cold. The most powerful clan on Earth was called Raven, and Ice Heart, chief of the Raven clan, kept the best of everything for himself. Blankets, baskets of food, and furs were piled high in his lodge, while his people went cold and hungry.

Ice Heart allowed no woman in his lodge, but his sister, Nushagak, who lived nearby, often prayed, "O great god Raven, please warm my brother's cold heart."

One day, when Ice Heart was hunting out in the midst of ice and snow, he came upon a dazzling maiden. When she smiled, light streamed from her eyes and all around. Ice Heart offered his arm. "Come with me, maiden. I am the great chief Ice Heart."

Smiling, the maiden glided along beside him in silence, lighting the way to the village. As she drew near, people came out of their lodges and crowded around her. The maiden's smiles warmed their hearts the way the sun warms the earth in spring. But Ice Heart pulled her into his lodge, slammed the door shut, and pointed to a pile of furs by the fire. "Sit there, maiden. You need not work, just save your smiles for me alone!"

"That I cannot do," she said, "for I smile on everyone alike."

"Smile on another soul and I'll bury you so deep in the earth that no one will ever see your smile!"

The maiden laughed. "Then you will lose my smile, but I will go on smiling."

In a rage, Ice Heart stormed out of his lodge and locked the door. He called a flock of little red birds. "Guard this rebellious woman. See that she smiles on no one while I am away!"

But no sooner had he gone hunting than the maiden went to the door and began to smile at all who passed by. Light streamed through cracks in the wood, warming the hearts of everyone in the village.

The little red birds raced off to tell the chief.

Back came Ice Heart, growling and cursing. He shoved the maiden into a great wooden chest and then lowered the chest into a space hidden beneath the floor of his lodge.

Suddenly the world felt colder and crueler than ever before.

Nushagak went to Ice Heart's door. "Release the maiden, brother. Surely Raven must frown at what you have done."

Up rose Ice Heart in a whirlwind of fury. He ordered Nushagak out of the village and then hacked her lodge to bits, even the totem pole with Raven carved on top.

Nushagak wandered through the snowfields until she came to the sea and could go no farther. Suddenly, she heard the beating of great wings.

The great god Raven landed before her. "Nushagak, you will give birth to a magical child. Raise the child properly and your people will be saved." Then Raven flew off.

Nushagak went into the woods, built a hut, and in ten days' time, she gave birth to a fine baby,

a boy she named Yehl, which means Helper. The child was one of the great-hearted spirits who are born whenever people's suffering is greatest.

In ten days' time, Yehl grew to the height of a man. Then Nushagak told him the secret of the maiden, blessed her son, and sent him to his uncle's lodge.

In those days, an uncle had to welcome his sister's children with honor, so Ice Heart gave Yehl food and a pile of furs to sleep on by the fire. But he swore to himself, "Surely my sister told the boy about the maiden. I must get rid of him."

The next morning, Ice Heart took the boy fishing and asked Yehl to stand on the bow of the canoe with his harpoon held high. Then Ice Heart rocked the boat, plunging the boy into the icy sea. Ice Heart paddled home, grinning gloomily.

That night, Yehl appeared at his uncle's door with a great string of fish slung over his shoulder.

"Why, nephew, I thought you had drowned. What a fine fisherman you are!" said Ice Heart. But he swore secretly, "I *must* get rid of him!"

The next morning, Ice Heart took Yehl to carve his new war canoe. Once the boy had climbed inside, Ice Heart sent down a huge tree trunk, smashing the canoe to bits and trapping Yehl inside. Ice Heart marched home, grinning gloomily.

Later that night, Ice Heart heard a knock at the door. There stood Yehl with a new war canoe on his shoulder, carved end to end with ravens.

Ice Heart's mouth twisted with rage. "Nephew, what a crafty carpenter you are!"

That night, as Yehl slept by the fire, Ice Heart crept toward him with his hunting knife held high, but he was stopped by a raven, who rose from the furs, cawing wildly and circling the lodge on great black wings.

"Oh no! He's Raven's child. I'm doomed," Ice Heart groaned. He raced up into the mountains to hide.

Then Yehl took his human form again, searched the lodge, and found the hidden space beneath the floor. He climbed down and felt around in the dark until he found a heavy wooden chest. When he lifted the lid, out flew a flock of tiny white birds, who swirled up through the smoke hole in the roof and out into the night sky, where they became the twinkling stars. Then Yehl felt a heavier chest, pulled open the lid, and up flew a silver bird, which soared out through the smoke hole to become the moon. When he pried open a third chest, the heaviest yet, up rose the maiden, smiling and beaming light all around.

"Well done, Yehl!" She rose into the sky to become the golden sun.

When Ice Heart saw the maiden's smile lighting up the whole sky, he became the Thunderbird, stirring up storm clouds to try and hide the maiden's smiles. But from that day to this, she always finds a way through the clouds to smile on everyone alike.

6. HOW THE SUN CAME

(Southern Georgia)

In the beginning, there was no light, no light anywhere on Earth. The first people, the animal people, were always stumbling around in the dark, bumping into the rocks and trees, and into each other.

"What we need," the big animals growled, "is some light!"

"Yes," cried the little animals. "What we need is light."

Finally, there got to be so many animals, and they all were bumping into each other so often, that they called a meeting in the dark to decide how to get some light.

The last to arrive was Red-headed Woodpecker. She flew in crying, "Light! I've seen light way over on the far side of the world!"

"Good, good!" said all the animals.

But then they began to fight about who should go to get the light. Who was the fastest? Who was the strongest? Who was the smartest?

Finally, Possum spoke up loudest of all. "I'm big! I'm strong! I've got sharp claws and the bushiest of all fur coats! I can hide the light in my fur!"

"Good, good!" cried all the animals.

So Possum set off in the darkness, traveling toward the Land of the Sun. As he got closer, Possum squinted his eyes to shut out the light, just as he does today. Then Possum grabbed a bit of sun and hid it in his fine thick, bushy tail, and back he went off through the darkness, all the way back to the Land of the Animal People.

He called out, "I'm back and I've brought you some light!"

"Good, good!" cried all the animals.

Possum reached for the light, but he discovered the sun had burnt off all the fur on his fine thick, bushy tail, and Possum's tail was as naked as it is today.

"Oh no!" cried Possum.

"Oh no!" cried all the animals. "Possum's lost all the fur on his fine thick, bushy tail, and still we have no light! What shall we do?"

Then Buzzard spoke up. "Awk! I'll bring you some light. Everybody knows my brain is very big. Look at all my fine thick head-feathers!"

"Good!" cried all the animals.

Buzzard set off through the darkness, flying high and straight as he does today. When he got to the Land of the Sun, Buzzard dove down, grabbed a bit of light, and hid it in his fine thick head-feathers. Then he flew back through the darkness to the Land of the Animal People.

"I've brought you some light!" Buzzard reached up and discovered that the sun had burnt off his fine thick head-feathers, and Buzzard's head was as naked as it is today. "AWK!"

"Oh no!" cried all the animals. "How will we get some light? We've sent our two best warriors!"

"You've done everything a warrior can do, it's true," said a tiny voice from down in the grass. "But perhaps this is something a little creature can do better than a big one."

The animals looked around. "Who are you, speaking to us in that funny little voice?"

"I am your Spider Grandmother. Perhaps I was put in the world to bring you light. Who knows? At least if I am burnt up, it's not as if you'll lose one of your big, strong warriors."

The animals were doubtful. What could a little spider do?

In the darkness, Spider Grandmother felt around until she found a lump of damp clay. She molded the clay into a bowl, a fine little round bowl. Holding up the bowl to dry and spinning a long thread out behind her, Spider Grandmother set off through the darkness, traveling toward the Land of the Sun.

When she arrived, Spider Grandmother grabbed a bit of the light, dropped it into her clay bowl, and traveled back along the thread she had spun. With light growing and spreading before her, Spider Grandmother returned to the land of the animal people, bringing with her the very first sunny day.

Ever since then, spiders have had the honor of spinning out webs in the shape of the rays of the sun.

How Is Everything Connected?

7. IDUNA AND THE MAGIC APPLES
(Scandinavia)

One day, Odin, the king of Heaven, wanted to go camping on Earth. His little brother, Loki, the god of fire, begged to go along. "I'll be good this time! No tricks, no lies. I'll even do all the cooking."

"All right, all right," said Odin.

Together, the brothers crossed the rainbow bridge from Heaven to Earth and camped on a green mountainside. That night, when Loki began to cook supper, his fire wouldn't stay lit. Then he saw the problem. From a branch above, an eagle was fanning down cold air. "If you want a hot supper, promise me some," the eagle croaked.

"All right, all right," said Loki.

But as soon as they began to eat, the eagle swooped down, snatched all the meat, and gobbled up every bit.

Loki grabbed a stick and smacked the eagle, but then the stick stuck to the eagle, and Loki's hands stuck to the stick. The eagle shot straight up into the sky, heading north and trailing Loki along. For the eagle was no eagle but Heaven's archenemy, the Frost Giant, in disguise.

"Let me go! Let me go! I'm freezing!" yelled Loki.

"On one condition!" roared the Frost Giant. "Bring Iduna and one of her apples outside Heaven's gate."

Nothing could be worse to ask, for Iduna, goddess of springtime, was the gardener of Heaven's orchard, where the apples of immortality grow, the apples that keep the gods and goddesses forever young. Yet through chattering teeth, Loki made the terrible promise. Then the Frost Giant dropped him on the ground.

Loki crossed the rainbow bridge to Heaven, but instead of confessing his terrible promise, he boasted to the gods and goddesses about how he had escaped from the Frost Giant's clutches.

The next day, after Iduna's mate, Braggi, the god of music and poetry, left with his harp to tune up the Earth's melodies, which were often out of harmony, Loki snuck into the orchard where Iduna danced among her apple trees, her green skirts flowing, her long braids flying.

"Iduna, there's something you should know. There's an apple tree with apples sweeter than yours."

"Sweeter? Impossible! Where?"

"Just outside Heaven's gate. Bring one of your apples and taste for yourself."

Iduna hurried after Loki, carrying her ripest, roundest, reddest apple in a crystal bowl. But no sooner had she set one foot outside Heaven's gate than the Frost Giant stormed down, swept her up, raced back to his frozen fortress in the north, and locked her in an ice cave.

"Now give me the apple!" the Frost Giant roared.

"Never," she replied.

"Give me the apple!" he hollered.

Again and again, Iduna refused.

Finally, in a fit of rage, the Frost Giant thrust his fist into the bowl and grabbed the apple. In that instant, the crystal bowl shattered and the apple turned to dust.

At the same time, in Heaven, all the apple trees in Iduna's orchard withered and all the apples fell to dust. All the gods and goddesses grew gray, sick, and bent. Braggi's harp cried tears.

On Earth, winter came and winter stayed. Leaves fell from the trees. Flowers faded. Birds and bees fell silent. Rivers froze. Nothing could grow. People grew sick, hungry, and frightened.

In Heaven, Odin called for a meeting, and everyone came except for Loki. Where was that trouble-maker? What had he done this time?

When he was dragged out of hiding, Loki whimpered, "But the Frost Giant said he only wanted one apple."

"Silence!" Odin commanded. "Bring back Iduna or be cursed forever as the traitor who destroyed Heaven and Earth."

Loki wandered off in shame.

Around a cloud came six gray cats pulling the cart of Freya, the goddess of love. Freya looked at Loki, her little brother, in pity. Trouble seemed to be glued to him. She wrapped her magic cloak of falcon feathers around Loki's shoulders. "Now, fly as a falcon to the Frost Giant's land, find Iduna, wrap her in my cloak, and fly back as fast as you can!"

So Loki flew to the frozen north, slipped between the bars of Iduna's ice cave, and wrapped her in Freya's cloak. Together, as falcons, they raced across the sky. All too soon, though, Loki and Iduna heard the Frost Giant howling after them and hurling huge hailstones. Ahead, Loki and Iduna could see the gods and goddesses watching. With the last of their strength, the gods and goddesses lit bonfires along the walls of Heaven.

Loki's strength was fading, so Iduna sang a song of spring to cheer him on, and Loki flew through the flames and skidded to a stop.

Unable to stop himself in time, the Frost Giant hit the walls of Heaven and shattered to bits, which quickly melted away.

Iduna leapt out of Freya's cape right into Braggi's arms. Sun burst through the clouds. Soon, ripe red apples covered the trees again, restoring health and happiness to all of Heaven. Harmony reigned once more.

Earth grew green again, too. Soon apple blossoms perfumed the air and apples covered the trees. Bees buzzed. Birds sang. Rivers ran.

But Loki's lies had caused such trouble that forever after he was known as Trickster Loki, so that Earth and Heaven alike might stay wise to his ways.

8. THE FIRST RAINBOW

(Northern California)

Atop the tallest tree in the forest, Spider Woman's web hung white with snow. Her sixty little spider children shivered as they slept. Snow had fallen every day for months. All the animals were cold, hungry, and frightened. Food supplies were almost gone. No one knew what to do.

Finally the animals decided to ask Coyote for help. "Coyote has been around since almost the beginning. He might know how to reach Silver Gray Fox, the creator, so we could beg him to end this terrible winter." They went to the cave where Coyote slept, woke him up, and asked.

Coyote growled, "Go away. Let me think." Then, after a short while, he stuck his head out into the cold air and sang to Silver Gray Fox, who lives above the clouds. Coyote yelped and yowled, but Silver Gray Fox didn't hear, or didn't want to. After all, Coyote's tricks and lies when the world was new had caused Silver Gray Fox to move away to live above the clouds. Coyote thought he'd better think some more.

Then he spotted Spider Woman swinging down on a silky thread from the top of the tallest tree in the forest. Spider Woman had been on Earth far longer than Coyote had. So Coyote yelped and yowled, "O Spider Woman! O wise one! We are all cold and hungry and afraid this winter will never end ever. Can you help?"

Spider Woman swayed her shining black body back and forth, back and forth, thinking and thinking. Her eight eyes sparkled when she finally spoke. "I know how to reach Silver Gray Fox, but I'm not the one for the work. You'll need my two littlest children. They're light as dandelion fluff, and they're the fastest spinners in my web." Spider Woman called them.

Spin! Spin! Down they came on their eight little legs, twin black spiders full of curiosity and fun.

"My dear little quick ones, are you ready for an adventure?" said Spider Woman.

"Yes! Yes!"

After Spider Woman explained her plan, the Spider Twins set off with Coyote in the snow. They hadn't gone far when they met the two White-footed Mouse Brothers rooting around for seeds.

Coyote told them of Spider Woman's plan. "Will you help?"

"Yes! Yes! We'll help!"

On the trail up Mount Shasta, they met Weasel Man, looking hungry and thinner than usual. Coyote told Weasel Man the plan. "Will you help?"

"Of course," he rasped.

Then they came across Red Fox Woman swishing her big fluffy tail through the bushes.

"Will you help?"

"Of course I will," she crooned.

Rabbit Woman poked her head out of her hole and sneezed, shivering despite her thick fur coat. "I'll come too."

Meadowlark wrapped her winter shawl around her wings and trudged after the others. At the top of Mount Shasta, the snow had stopped, but the sky was still cloudy and the air was ice cold.

Coyote barked orders. "Will our archers step forward?" The two White-footed Mouse Brothers lifted their bows.

"Ready? One!"

All the animals drew in deep breaths.

"Two!"

The White-footed Mouse Brothers pulled back their bowstrings.

"Three!"

Both arrows shot straight up and hit the same spot in the clouds and stuck there. Then the White-footed Mouse Brothers, Red Fox Woman, and Coyote sang as loudly as they could. Rabbit Woman sang and shook her rattle. Weasel Man sang and beat his old, worn elk-hide drum. The Spider Twins spun out long, long lines of spider silk as fast as they could.

All the singing lifted up the spider silk until the lines caught onto the arrows stuck in the same spot in the clouds. Then the Spider Twins scurried up the lines of silk and disappeared through the hole in the sky.

When Silver Gray Fox spied the little spiders scrambling through the clouds, he demanded, "What are you two doing here?"

The Spider Twins bent low on their eight legs. "O Silver Gray Fox, greetings from our mother, Spider Woman, and all the creatures below. Please will you let the sun shine again? Everyone's cold and hungry and afraid that winter will never end."

The Spider Twins spoke so politely that Silver Gray Fox said more gently, "How did you two get up here?"

"Do you hear everyone singing, and the drum and rattle? Our mother made a plan."

Silver Gray Fox nodded. "You all worked together, even that rascal Coyote? Your mother made a

good plan. As a reward, you may help me create a sign that spring will come. First, picture a beam of sunlight curving across the damp sky."

The twins thought hard, and a golden beam curved across the sky.

"Now, picture stripes of red and of blue on either side."

The Spider Twins thought hard and the stripes appeared.

"Now, in between, add stripes of orange, violet, and green."

The Spider Twins stared at the glowing arch of colors in the sky.

Then Silver Gray Fox told the Spider Twins to fasten the ends of the rainbow to Earth in secret. After all that work, the Spider Twins' legs ached.

Down on Earth, under the clouds, the singing had stopped. The animals were colder, hungrier, and more worried than ever. Spider Woman missed her two youngest children. Each day she missed them more.

When the Spider Twins spun back down to Earth, Spider Woman wrapped all eight legs around her two littlest children. Their fifty-eight sisters and brothers jumped up and down with joy.

As the clouds began to drift apart, sunlight reached the damp air.

"Look up!" the Spider Twins cried.

There was the very first rainbow. As the Sun began to warm the air again, grass pushed up its pale green arms through the melting snow. Meadowlark blew her silver whistle of spring across the valleys, calling streams and rivers awake. Coyote raced to a hilltop and gave a howl of joy.

The animals held a feast in honor of Spider Woman, the Spider Twins, and all the hard work everyone had done. Now on wet mornings, tiny rainbows shine inside the dewdrops hanging on spider webs. That is the spider's special reward.

9. MONKEY KING

(China)

Long ago in China, an emperor guarded each of Heaven's gates, but at the south gate, the youngest emperor could not sit still. He always jumped off his throne and ran about looking for new amusements. One day, he stumbled on a stone shaped like a monkey. Using his heavenly powers, he stirred the stone to life.

All at once, a magical monkey appeared, jumped from Heaven to Earth, and walked on the sea. Then he strode over the clouds and rode the winds back to Heaven. The young emperor watched, wide-eyed.

All the monkeys on Earth watched too, and chattered in amazement. "Monkey King! Monkey King!"

Monkey liked being called Monkey King, and he liked having an army of followers. But before long, he grumbled, "Monkey King? Monkey King? Not good enough. What I should be is Monkey God!" He snooped all around to find whatever might give him more power. Monkey even went down to the underwater realm of the sea dragons to ask, "What is the most wondrous thing in your kingdom?"

Proudly, Sea Dragon King brought out a magic wand. "This wand can grow or shrink to any size, and it makes wishes come true."

Monkey grabbed the wand and fled, pulling precious silks and pearls from the gardens of the sea as he went. He reappeared on land dressed in such splendor that seven warlords held a feast in his honor, but at the feast, Monkey ate and drank so much that he fell asleep on the table.

The sea dragon army stormed in, grabbed Monkey, dragged him down to hell, locked him up, and wrote his name in the Book of Judgment. But with the magic wand hidden behind his ear, Monkey soon escaped, and he erased his name from the Book of Judgment as he went.

Now Monkey felt afraid of no one. He shouted up to Heaven, "Now make me Monkey God!"

Hoping to keep Monkey from causing more mischief, the gods and goddesses offered him the job of a minor god: stable keeper of the heavenly horses.

Mucking out smelly stables? Not good enough! Monkey had a tantrum. He cursed his creator. He even tried kicking down Heaven's south gate. The terrified young emperor begged the gods and goddesses for help. In desperation, they offered Monkey a more important job as gardener of the peach orchard where the peaches grew that kept the goddesses and gods forever young. This was indeed a great honor.

Monkey accepted, and all was well for a time. The heavenly peaches grew sweet and ripe. But before long, Monkey muttered, "Monkey God? Monkey God? Not good enough! What I should be is ruler of Heaven!"

Then Monkey found out he wasn't even invited to the heavenly peach festival, the most important feast of the year. So on the day of the feast, Monkey hid under the table, and using the magic

wand, he put all the goddesses and gods to sleep. Then he jumped up and ate every one of the heavenly peaches and drank every drop of the peach wine.

Staggering home, Monkey wandered into the garden of the wizard Lao Chun, who was asleep at the feast. Lao Chun had just invented an elixir of immortality, so Monkey snooped around until he found the elixir hidden inside a gourd, and then he drank every drop. Now Monkey was twice immortal.

When the gods and goddesses awoke and found that all the peaches were gone, saw Monkey's paw prints on the plates, and heard that Lao Chun's elixir was missing, they captured Monkey. They dragged him back to Lao Chun's garden and begged the wizard to change Monkey into some other—any other!—form.

Lao Chun shoved Monkey into his alchemical oven and locked the lid. For forty-nine days and forty-nine nights the oven burnt at white-hot heat. On the fiftieth day, the wizard lifted the lid.

Monkey leapt out, unchanged. "Now make me ruler of Heaven."

In despair, the goddesses and gods called on Buddha for help.

Buddha asked Monkey, "Why do you think that you should rule Heaven?"

"Why? Because I can ride the winds, stride the clouds, and walk the seas. In a single jump, I can leap the world and Heaven, too. And I have a magic wand that makes wishes come true. And I have an army of followers who call me Monkey King."

"True," said Buddha. "But there are greater powers and bigger armies. What other powers do you possess?"

"I ate all the heavenly peaches and drank all of Lao Chun's elixir, so I'm twice immortal, twice as good as any god. Twice as good as you!"

"I see," said Buddha. "Then if you can escape my reach, I will make you ruler of Heaven."

With that, Monkey leapt across the world, landed at the base of one of the four pillars that hold up the sky, and made his secret mark at the base of the third pillar. In a single jump, he returned to Buddha. "Now make me ruler of Heaven!"

Buddha held up his hand. "Foolish one, that cannot be, for you have not yet left the palm of my hand." Monkey shook with fear. There was his secret mark at the base of Buddha's third finger.

Buddha then fitted Monkey with a helmet that would tighten if he even *thought* of doing mischief. And Monkey earned a new title, the god of victorious struggle, for he had won the hardest battle of all: to manage his own nature. And finally Heaven's youngest emperor learned to sit still and meditate, and Heaven was peaceful—at least for a little while each day.

10. THE PERILOUS POMEGRANATE

(Greece)

Long ago, the goddess Demeter came down from Heaven to care for all life on Earth. Of her many children, Demeter's favorite was Persephone. Flowers burst into bloom in Persephone's footsteps wherever she danced, and she danced wherever she went.

Bees buzzed. Birds sang. Rivers ran. There was food enough for all. Earth was more like Heaven then.

But one afternoon, Persephone didn't come home. Demeter waited till long after dark. Then she went out across the fields, searching and calling, "Persephone! Persephone?" But she found no trace of the girl, and no one knew—at least wouldn't say—where she went. By morning, Demeter knew something terrible had happened. Flower petals lay all over the ground. The air had lost its sweetness.

"Persephone? Persephone?" cried Demeter as she staggered across the countryside. Sorrow snapped like a wolf at her heart. Crops withered and turned to dust. Birds and bees fell silent. Nothing could grow while the mother of all things grieved. Winter came and winter stayed. Hunger and sickness came, too.

Then one cold midnight at a crossroads, Demeter met Hecate, the old goddess of death, holding her lantern high to light the way for lost souls.

"O Hecate, can you tell me where is my Persephone?"

Hecate pointed a bony finger straight down. "Persephone went to hell, she did, in the chariot of the bully who stole my throne and made me homeless. Hades stole your daughter. He takes whatever he wants!"

"Hades! My own brother? What are you saying?"

"Persephone was dancing up some new red poppies when Hades drove his chariot below and caught a whiff of the sweetness above. He caused an earthquake that cracked open the ground, then he drove up, grabbed the girl, and raced back down."

"And how is my daughter?"

"Hades has crowned her queen of the dead and put her on my old black marble throne, but Persephone does not smile or speak or eat. She just sits there, so sad, so pale, so thin."

With that, Demeter whirled around, stormed up Mount Olympus, and burst into the golden bedroom of her brother Zeus, king of the gods.

"Wake up, brother! Hades has stolen Persephone and made her his queen. Make him return my daughter at once!"

Now, Zeus had seen Hades steal Persephone but said nothing. Zeus yawned. "Why get so upset, sister?"

"I will not live without my daughter."

"But Hades has made your girl a queen."

"Queen of the dead, and it's killing me. And if I die, Earth dies. And then there will be no one left to worship us, so all of Heaven will die, too!"

Zeus rolled over and yawned again. "You and the girl were so close, sister. Perhaps it's time you let her grow up."

With that, Demeter hurled a hailstorm down onto Heaven's floor, the first that had ever fallen there. Snow and sleet slid across the shining marble slabs. "Make Hades return Persephone *or else.*" She stormed back down Mount Olympus.

Zeus tossed off his silken bedcovers, got up, and looked down. Earth was gray and grim indeed. People were so cold and hungry they had stopped taking offerings to the temples. Zeus scribbled a hasty note to his brother, Hades, and ordered his messenger, Iris, the rainbow, to take the message to the underworld.

When Hades read his brother Zeus's note, he swore every curse ever grown in his garden of curses and even made up some new ones. Hades hated having to give in to Demeter, or to any woman. He pushed through the dead spirits whispering in the dark like bugs in compost and went to the black marble throne where Persephone sat silent, rocking to her own private music.

"Well, my young queen, this isn't quite as romantic as I'd hoped."

Persephone's eyes flew open.

"You may return to your mother's realm, after all."

Persephone's heart leapt with joy.

"You'll need strength for the journey. Here, my dear." Hades held out a handful of pomegranate seeds.

Persephone took four seeds, swallowed them, and quickly licked the blood-red juice from her fingers. Then she hurried away after Iris without a word of farewell or a backward glance.

Hades gave a cruel grin as he watched her go.

At dawn, Iris the rainbow cast her radiant band of colors across the sky, and Persephone climbed out of the underworld. As soon as her feet touched Earth again, flowers burst into bloom. Warmth and sweetness filled the air again, waking Demeter, who rushed outside.

Persephone danced right into her mother's arms. Health and happiness returned to the Mother of All Things. Bees buzzed, birds sang, rivers ran. Earth grew green again.

All too soon, however, Demeter learned of Hades's cruel trick. Persephone, not knowing that pomegranate seeds were the food of the dead, had swallowed four in all. For the four seeds she had swallowed, Persephone would have to return to the underworld for four months each year. So it was that this first spring was only the first, and that first winter, when Demeter had turned Earth gray and grim, was not the last. From then on, mother and daughter would be parted again and again, but only for a portion of each year.

Persephone now spends the winter months in the underworld in a deep, deep sleep, dreaming up new flowers.

Demeter endures winters more calmly now, too. She designs new plantings, prunes her fruit trees, and curls up with garden books, dreaming of spring.

11. MOTHER HOLLE

(Germany)

Once there were two sisters. One was a hard worker, the other was lazy, so the hardworking girl had to do all the cleaning and cooking of the house. After doing all her chores, the hardworking girl would go out to sit by the well near her house and weave and spin yarn until her fingers bled. One afternoon, as she dipped the sharp wooden shuttle into the well to wash off a drop of blood, the shuttle fell from her hand and sank to the bottom. She ran home crying and told her sister.

"Since you let the shuttle fall in, you must get it out again," said the sister.

So the hardworking girl went to the well and jumped in. Down, down, down she sank. When she reached the bottom, she couldn't find the shuttle, but she felt a door and opened it. Through it there was a meadow of golden wheat, with sunny blue skies overhead. The girl walked through the wheat until she came to an oven that smelled of hot bread.

She heard the bread cry out, "Oh, help! Help us, please! Take us out or we shall burn!"

The girl took out the loaves and left them to cool in the shade.

Then she came to an apple tree that called, "Oh, shake me, shake me or my branches will break!

My apples are ripe and heavy!"

The girl shook the tree till apples fell like rain. She gathered the apples into a heap and went on.

At last she came to a little house where an old woman was working out in the garden. "Come in, lass," the woman said with a smile.

The woman had such great big teeth that the girl pulled back in fear.

"There's nothing to fear, lass. Work for me and you shall be the better for it. Your job will be to shake my bedcovers every day until the feathers fly and then there is snow upon Earth, for I am Mother Holle, keeper of the seasons."

Mother Holle spoke so kindly that the girl agreed to stay and work for her. Each day, she shook the bedcovers until the feathers flew and then there was snow upon Earth. She had a pleasant time at Mother Holle's house, with never a cross word.

After three months' time, though, the girl grew lonely for her own world and told Mother Holle that she would like to leave.

"You have served me well, and I am pleased, so I shall see you out," said Mother Holle. She led the girl back to the door of the well at the edge of the meadow. As she walked through the door, a shower of gold rained down all over the girl's clothes.

"You have that gold because you worked so hard," said Mother Holle, and she gave the girl back her shuttle.

Then the girl closed the door and floated up the well until she reached the top. As she approached her old home, the rooster crowed, "Cockadoodledoo, cockadoodledoo! Your golden girl's come back to you!"

The lazy sister ran out and marveled at the sight of all the gold. Right away, she asked the girl where she had been. When she heard, the lazy sister said, "Then I shall have some gold, too!"

But no spinning for her! She grabbed the shuttle, went to the well, and pricked her hand till a drop of blood fell into the water. She threw in the shuttle, jumped in, and sank to the bottom. She opened the door, walked into the meadow, and came to the oven.

The bread cried out, "Oh, help! Help! Take us out or we shall burn!"

The girl snorted. "Why should I get hot and dirty for you?"

She went on and came to the apple tree, which cried out, "Oh, shake me, shake me or my branches will break! My apples are ripe and heavy!"

"No, thank you! What if your apples fell on my head?"

The lazy girl went straight to Mother Holle's house, and she was not afraid because she had already heard about the woman's great big teeth. At once, she agreed to work for Mother Holle.

The first day, the lazy girl forced herself to work hard, thinking of the gold. She shook Mother Holle's bedcovers till the feathers flew and there was snow upon Earth. Mother Holle was pleased. But the second day, the lazy girl woke up late, and the third day she didn't get up until noon.

Mother Holle was soon tired of this and told the lazy girl that she could leave. As Mother Holle led her to the door to the well at the edge of the meadow, the lazy girl thought of all the gold to come. But as she walked through, a shower of smelly, greenish pine pitch spilled over her.

"That is your reward," said Mother Holle. The door closed.

The lazy girl kicked her way up the well and climbed out.

The rooster cried, "Cockadoodledoo, cockadoodledoo! Your pitchy girl's come back to you!"

The pitch stuck fast to the lazy girl for a long, long time and could not be scrubbed off no matter how hard her hardworking sister tried.

12. MARUSHKA AND THE TWELVE MONTHS (Romania)

Once upon a time, there was once a woman who had two daughters: Holena, whom she loved, and Marushka, whom she couldn't stand—even though Marushka did all the housework all day long, while Holena ordered her sister about and gazed in the mirror trying to improve her appearance. "Marushka, brush my hair! Marushka, make my bed! Marushka, sweep my room!"

In spite of all the hard work, or perhaps because of it, Marushka grew lovelier day by day. And in spite of her lazy life, or perhaps because of it, Holena grew sourer and sourer.

One cold January day, when snow covered the ground, Holena thought she could not stand another moment with her hardworking, lovely sister. "Stop cleaning, Marushka! Go into the woods and find me some violets!"

"But, sister, whoever heard of violets growing in the snow?"

"Find some violets and don't come back until you do!"

Holena took Marushka by the shoulders and pushed her out the door.

Thick white snow covered the ground. Marushka shivered as the afternoon faded into night, and as she walked she grew frightened. At last, she saw a faint light on a mountainside, so she decided to climb up to it. When she arrived she found a great fire surrounded by twelve stones, with one taller than the rest. On each stone, a person sat facing the flames.

Marushka stepped forward. "Greetings, good souls. Please may I warm myself by your fire?"

The tall, white-haired man on the highest stone motioned Marushka closer. "Welcome, Marushka. We are the twelve months, and I am January. But why are you out in the snow alone and so late, my dear?"

"My sister, Holena, says I must get her some violets. Do you know where I might find any?"

January got off the rock and walked over to the rock upon which sat a smiling curly-haired boy. The old man handed him a wand. "Here, March, you take the high seat."

So March climbed onto the high stone and waved the wand over the fire. Flames blazed up and the snow melted away. Pink and blue violets sprang up until it looked as if a flowered quilt lay on the ground.

Marushka thanked March, gathered up a bunch of violets, and hurried home.

Imagine Holena's surprise when she saw Marushka. "Where did you find the violets?"

"High in the mountains, the ground was covered with them."

Without a word of thanks, Holena snatched the violets, pinned them to her dress, and sniffed their sweet fragrance all day. The next day, Holena ordered, "Stop cleaning, Marushka! Get me some strawberries!"

"Strawberries! But, sister, whoever heard of strawberries growing in the snow?"

"Bring me some strawberries and don't come back until you do!"

So Marushka again climbed up the snowy mountain to the stone circle around the fire.

January sighed, "What does Holena want today, Marushka?"

"She wants strawberries. Do you know where I might find any?"

January handed the wand to June, a rosy-cheeked woman with long yellow braids. "Here, June, you take the high seat."

June took the high seat and waved the wand over the fire. Flames blazed up and snow melted away. Starry white blossoms and little green leaves popped up, then turned into fruit, first green, then pink, and then became ripe red strawberries.

Marushka thanked June, filled her apron with berries, and hurried home.

Imagine Holena's surprise when she saw the strawberries. "Where did you get them?"

"Up the mountain, the ground was covered with them."

Without a word of thanks, Holena gobbled up the berries. But the next afternoon, she ordered, "Stop cleaning, Marushka. Get me some apples!"

"Sister, who ever heard of apples growing in the snow?"

"Get me some apples and don't come back until you do!" Holena took Marushka by the shoulders and shoved her out into the snow.

Again Marushka climbed up the mountain.

January growled, "What does Holena want now?"

"Apples."

January handed the wand to a woman with brown braids streaked with gray. "September, you take the high seat." September waved the wand, the fire blazed up, the snow melted away, and an apple tree sprang up covered with ripe red apples. Marushka picked two, thanked September, and hurried home.

Holena and her mother were more surprised than ever to see Marushka coming in from the snow with apples. "Where did you get them?"

"High on the mountain, there is a tree covered with apples."

Holena grabbed one, and her mother grabbed the other. They declared that they'd never tasted anything so good. No sooner were they done than they both wanted more. "Mother, get my fur cloak. We are going ourselves this time," said Holena. They rushed out into the snow and climbed up the mountain, determined to get more apples. They came to the stone circle and went to the fire to warm themselves without a word of greeting.

Old January glowered. "Who are you?"

"What business is that of yours, you old fool?" said Holena, who was looking for the apple tree.

January's frown grew deeper. He waved the wand over his own head, and the fire died down. Icy wind slashed across the mountain. Snow kept falling, fast and thick. Wind kept blowing. Soon Holena and her mother could not see one step ahead.

Back at home, Marushka cooked dinner and waited, but her mother and Holena didn't come down that night, and they never did come. In spring, when the snow melted, she found two new stones on the mountain, leaning together like two pieces of a broken heart. Marushka lived a long and happy life, always grateful to all twelve months of the year.

13. PSYCHE: A STORY OF THE SOUL

(Greece)

Princess Psyche was as kind and gentle as she was beautiful. Men feared to court her, and women feared to befriend her. Everyone worshipped Psyche from afar. Her only friends were the creatures of the palace garden—the bugs and birds, plants and stones.

When reports of Psyche's beauty reached all the way to Mount Olympus, Aphrodite, the goddess of beauty, grew ragingly jealous. "A mortal as beautiful as me? Impossible! I had better put a stop to that, otherwise people will be building temples to the silly little mortal."

Aphrodite called her son Eros, god of desire. "Fly to Earth, my darling boy, and prick Psyche's heart with one of your magic arrows, so that she'll fall in love with the first man—preferably a hideous one—who comes along. That will take care of that!"

Eros flew straight to his target, took one look at Psyche and, for the first time in his life, fell head over wings in love. To escape his mother's jealousy, Eros begged South Wind to carry Psyche away to a silver pavilion in a faraway valley. Every night, Eros flew in to wake Psyche with a kiss. In the dark, he made her laugh with his promises of bliss and warmed her lonely heart. "All I ask," said Eros, "is that you never look at me." Eros wanted to test Psyche, to be sure that he could trust her, for trust is the basis for love.

So Psyche promised. Night after night they spent in bliss, and day after day they spent apart. In time, though, Psyche's curiosity could not be contained. She had felt Eros's feathered wings and thick curls, but what if his face was motley blue or who knows what? One night, as he slept, Psyche raised an oil lamp over the bed, and when she at last saw her lover's face, she pulled back in surprise. He was no monster but the loveliest white-feather-winged, golden-skinned boy imaginable. As Psyche pulled back, a drop of hot oil spilled from the lamp onto Eros's arm.

"Ow, you hurt me! And you broke your promise!" cried Eros. "Love cannot live where there is no trust."

"I'm sorry! I took only a peek."

As Eros flew off, the silver pavilion vanished. Psyche found herself alone in a barren wilderness.

Up on Mount Olympus, furious Aphrodite took in her heart-broken son. To punish Psyche, Aphrodite sent her handmaidens Sadness and Sorrow to heap up a mountain of seeds from every plant on Earth. Then Aphrodite herself appeared to Psyche. "Sort these seeds each into its own kind by nightfall or die, wicked girl."

"O goddess of beauty, have mercy on me!"

Aphrodite showed none.

But a friendly ant heard Psyche's cry and called all the ants around to come and sort the seeds into each kind. By nightfall, the task was done.

In a rage at having been bested, Aphrodite set Psyche a worse challenge the next day. "Go to the pasture by the river, disobedient girl, and gather golden fleece from the sheep that graze there. I need a new shawl for the nights I spend with my wounded son."

Psyche shuddered. Not only did the sheep have golden fleece but also golden horns, golden hooves, and golden teeth, which could tear a person to bits. She sank to her knees in despair.

A friendly reed at the river's edge whispered, "Psyche, Psyche, Psyche, wait until midday when the sheep seek shade in the woods, then pluck the golden fleece they leave on the bushes." And so Psyche did, much to Aphrodite's extreme displeasure.

The next day, Aphrodite handed Psyche a golden box and a task meant to be the last. "Go down to Hades, wretched girl, and ask the queen of the dead for some of her elixir of beauty, for I have lost some of mine in tending my wounded son!"

Knowing that no mortal had ever returned from the Land of the Dead, Psyche climbed up a stone tower for one last look at Earth, ready to leap off. But the stones of the tower rumbled, "Go, Psyche, and stop for nothing and no one. Do only what Aphrodite asked."

So Psyche took the long, gloomy path down into the underworld. At the entrance, she met the Fates, three old women. One spins the thread of each life, one measures it out, and one cuts off its length. "Come, Psyche, see the destiny we weave for you," they called.

Psyche ached to know if she would ever see Eros again, but instead of following the Fates, she forced one foot ahead of the other all the way to the palace where Persephone, queen of the underworld, sat silent on a black marble throne.

With trembling hands, Psyche held out Aphrodite's golden box.

Silent and slow as a snake, Persephone filled the box with some of her elixir of dreams and sleep's deep forgetfulness.

Then Psyche retraced her path up to Earth. But, just before stepping out into daylight, she stopped, feeling weary to the bone. "I must need a bit of the elixir, too." No sooner had she opened the box a crack, not knowing it was too strong for any mortal, Psyche fell to the ground, pale as death.

Just then, Eros, his wounded heart having healed at last, happened to be out testing his wings. When he saw Psyche on the ground, he flew to her side and brought her to life with a kiss. After many more kisses, Psyche and Eros pledged to love each other forever, even though marriage between gods and mortals was forbidden. Psyche then went off to deliver the elixir to Aphrodite, and Eros raced to see Zeus, king of Heaven, to beg him for help.

When Zeus heard of Psyche's courageous devotion, he, for the first time ever, offered a sip of the elixir of immortality to a mortal. With one sip, Psyche gained the first human soul. Ever since, each mortal is born with a soul that never dies. The word *psyche* means "soul" in Greek.

All of Heaven and Earth rejoiced at the marriage of Psyche and Eros. Even Aphrodite, more beautiful than ever, danced at their wedding. When Psyche and Eros had a child, they named her Bliss.

Why Are We Here?

14. THE OLD WOMAN WHO LIVED IN A VINEGAR BOTTLE (England)

Once there was a fairy who flew north, south, east, and west, all about the business fairies do best: casting spells, granting wishes, and stirring up mischief here and there. One day, she heard a little voice coming from a vinegar bottle. She stopped and listened, and what do you think she heard? Why, the voice of a little old woman.

"It's a shame! It's a shame! It's a shame! I shouldn't live in this vinegar bottle. What I should have is a cozy cottage in the country with roses climbing up the walls."

With a smile, the fairy waved her wand. "Very well. Turn 'round three times when you go to bed tonight, and see what you see by morning light."

The old woman turned 'round three times, went straight to bed, and in the morning when she woke up, she was in a cozy cottage with roses climbing up the walls, and she was very happy, but she quite forgot to thank the fairy.

The fairy flew north, south, east, and west, all about the business fairies do best. Then she flew to the window of the rose-covered cottage, and what do you think she heard?

"It's a shame! It's a shame! It's a shame! I shouldn't live in this tiny cottage. What I should have is a big city house with lace curtains at the windows and people living up and down the street."

With a sigh, the fairy waved her wand. "Very well. Turn 'round three times when you go to bed tonight, and see what you see by morning light."

The old woman turned 'round three times, went straight to bed, and in the morning when she woke up, she was in a big city house with lace curtains at the windows and people living up and down the street, but she quite forgot to thank the fairy.

The fairy flew north, south, east, and west, all about the business fairies do best. Then she flew to the big city house, listened at the lace-curtained window, and what do you think she heard?

"It's a shame! It's a shame! It's a shame! I shouldn't live in this city house. I should be queen of a golden castle, with a golden crown and a golden throne and people to order about all day long!"

With a frown, the fairy waved her wand. "Very well. Turn 'round three times when you go to bed tonight and see what you see by morning light."

So the old woman turned 'round three times, went straight to bed, and in the morning when she woke up she was queen of a golden castle, with a golden crown, a golden throne, and people to order about all day long, which she did. But she quite forgot to thank the fairy.

The fairy flew north, south, east, and west, all about the business fairies do best. Then she flew to the window of the golden castle, and what do you think she heard?

"It's a shame! It's a shame! It's a shame! I shouldn't be queen of this castle. What I should be is ruler of the whole round world!"

With a curious grin, the fairy waved her wand. "Very well. Turn 'round three times when you go to bed tonight and see what you see by morning light."

So the old woman turned 'round three times, went straight to bed, and in the morning when she woke up, she was back in her vinegar bottle.

15. CLOUDSPINNER AND THE HUNGRY SERPENT (Japan)

Long ago in Japan, while Yosaku the farmer was weeding his cabbage patch, he noticed a serpent about to strike a beautiful silver-and-black spider. Yosaku brought his hoe down hard, missing the serpent but frightening it away. As he did so, Yosaku ripped his old cotton kimono—his only one, for he was very poor.

The silver-and-black spider hurried away and hid behind a cabbage.

Yosaku went home to his little hut, had a bowl of rice—for that was all he had—and went to sleep. But before morning light, he heard a voice calling, "Yosaku, Yosaku." He looked out the window.

There stood a beautiful maiden in a silver-and-black kimono. "Let me in. I've come to weave for you, Yosaku."

So Yosaku let the maiden in and led her to his dusty weaving room, which held only a small bundle of cotton and a dusty loom. The maiden went in and shut the door, and Yosaku went off to tend his cabbages.

When he returned that evening, to his amazement, a brand new cotton kimono sat on his table, neatly folded. Yosaku thanked the maiden and asked what he might do for her.

"The only thing I ask is that you never come into the weaving room while I am working."

"As you wish, maiden."

Each day, Yosaku placed a tray of rice cakes and tea outside the weaving room door, but when he returned, nothing had been touched. Yet, each day, the maiden emerged from the weaving room with a new kimono, until Yosaku's chest was stacked high.

One day, Yosaku's curiosity could not be contained. He crept to the window of the weaving room and peered in. There he saw no maiden at the loom but a beautiful silver-and-black spider—the same spider he had saved from the serpent. She would eat the cotton, spin the cotton into thread, and weave the thread into cloth.

Right away, Yosaku piled his cart high with cabbages and set off for town and sold them to buy more cotton so that the spider maiden would never go hungry. Then he put his big new bundle of cotton into his cart. But on the way home, when Yosaku stopped to tend his cabbages, the serpent slithered into the cart and hid inside the bundle of cotton.

Yosaku reached home and left the bundle of cotton just outside the weaving room door. No sooner had the spider maiden opened the door to pull in the new cotton, however, than out slithered the serpent, rattling its tail and hissing hungrily.

The spider maiden screamed and leapt out the window. The serpent followed, jaws opened wide. The spider maiden ran and ran, but the serpent kept slithering after her faster and faster.

Yosaku grabbed his hoe and chased after the serpent. And then, just as the serpent was about to trap the maiden in his fangs, she spun up a long, long line of spider silk and caught it onto a sunbeam. Then she scrambled up the line, lifting herself out of the serpent's reach and into the sky.

The serpent hissed angrily and slithered away, hungry and mad.

Yosaku watched in delight as the spider maiden began to spin soft, fluffy, white cottony clouds in the sky. To this day in Japan, the same word is used for both "spider" and "cloud": *kumo*.

16. THE LOST SPEAR
(South Africa)

Once upon a time in Africa, a bright-eyed, beautiful princess called Lala decided she wanted a hut of her own and a mate. She told her father, the chief, that she wished to find the kindest, bravest, and handsomest man in the land. Lala's father was angry. He did not want his daughter to choose a mate for herself. He wanted the strongest man in the land to rule her and the people, as he always had, by force.

So the chief called for a contest to see which man might throw the *assegi,* a long spear, the farthest.

Four young men came to try. Three were the sons of rich and powerful families, and one was a poor herdsman called Zandele. He stood tall and handsome and had the kindest brown eyes.

Right away, Lala liked Zandele the best. The people did, too.

On the day of the contest, the three rich young men threw their spears first, and they threw far. Then Zandele threw, and he threw farthest of all.

The people cheered, "Zandele's won!"

Lala laughed with joy and told her father, "Zandele is the man I want."

But the chief was angry and unjust. He did not want his daughter to pick a poor herdsman when three perfectly good rich men were right at hand. He demanded another contest. "Let all four men throw again, this time using my spears."

Four gold spears that looked exactly alike were brought from the royal treasury, but the king's magician had hexed the spear given to Zandele.

Again the four young men threw. And again the first three threw first and far. Then Zandele threw, and his spear overshot all the others—but it kept going and going and finally disappeared in the clouds over a distant mountain.

"If you wish to look upon my daughter ever again, bring back the royal spear," said the chief.

With a heavy heart, Zandele said farewell to Lala and set off toward the mountain where the spear had vanished.

On the first day of his travels, a bird clutching a tiny green frog in its beak fell at Zandele's feet. Zandele set the little frog free.

The frog croaked, "If ever you need help, call me to mind and I shall come."

Zandele smiled, thanked the little frog, and went on.

On the second day, he came upon a beautiful black-and-yellow butterfly that was impaled on a thornbush. He stopped and set the butterfly free.

"You are kind, Zandele, and I am thankful," fluttered the butterfly. "If ever you need help, call me to mind and I shall come."

Zandele smiled, thanked the butterfly, and went on.

On the third night, as the moon rose full and blood red, he made his way up a narrow canyon where a stream flowed along. As he passed a pool of water, he saw a little gray spider swimming with all its might, but sinking. He lifted the spider out and set it to dry on a rock.

The spider bowed on its eight little legs. "Thank you, Zandele! If ever you need help, call me to mind and I shall come."

Zandele smiled, thanked the spider, and went on until he came to a cave where he slept. In the middle of the night, he awoke to the sound of strange, sweet music coming from deep in the cave. As he crept toward the sound, the music grew louder and sweeter. The light grew brighter.

Then around a corner, Zandele came upon a dazzling sight. A vast cavern sparkled all over with diamonds, rubies, and emeralds. In the middle was a lake of sapphire blue, where moon fairies with starflower wreaths in their hair floated along, singing and glowing with light.

Then the music stopped.

A voice called out from the middle of the lake. "Welcome to the Land of the Moon Fairies, Zandele. We've been expecting you."

"You have?"

"Have no fear, Zandele. The royal spear is within your reach. Come closer."

A golden canoe came to a stop at Zandele's feet. He stepped in, and the canoe carried him out to a throne carved of one huge emerald. There sat the queen of the moon fairies.

"Zandele, a task awaits you before you may claim the royal spear. You must make lively the one dull chamber of our realm. Do this or death will be your doom, for that is our law."

Then the canoe took Zandele across the lake to an empty chamber whose walls, floor, and ceiling were all of mud. Nothing but cold, gray mud.

Despair filled Zandele's heart, for he had nothing with which to make the place beautiful. At the thought of never seeing Lala again, Zandele fell to his knees and wept until he fell asleep.

When he awoke and opened his eyes, Zandele stared about in amazement. The spider and her

many children, the butterfly and her sisters and brothers, and the little green frog and all his tribe had come and turned the muddy room into a radiant space of shimmering silver spider webs, black-and-yellow butterfly wings, and tiny emerald-green frogs.

The queen and her moon fairies rushed in to see and laughed in delight. "He's won! Zandele's won the royal spear!"

Zandele claimed his prize. In no time, he was back before the hut of the king, and he threw down the lost spear.

Beautiful, black-eyed Lala rushed out of her father's house, laughing with joy, and danced right into Zandele's arms. "Not only are you the strongest man in the land, you are the kindest, bravest, and wisest. I choose you as my mate."

The people cheered.

The king retired to his hut, looking angry and extremely unwell, and he never did come out again.

So with Zandele by her side, Lala took the throne and ruled wisely and well for a long, long time. Happiness filled the land.

17. THE LITTLE MAN NO BIGGER THAN YOUR THUMB WITH MUSTACHES SEVEN MILES LONG (Russia)

Long ago in a green valley, Queen Wiseheart gave birth to twin daughters. She and King Wiseheart were so pleased that they named them Loveliness that Shines and Jewel without a Price. Soon, the parents began to worry about how to protect their daughters, so they built a high wall around the palace, then a higher one, and then a higher one still. Even so, they worried, so they hired seventy-seven indoor nurses, seventy-seven outdoor nurses, and seventy-seven guards to guard the walls.

One day, Loveliness that Shines and Jewel without a Price were out in the garden picking flowers when a whirling cloud of shadow and light swept down and blinded the nurses and guards. When the whirlwind vanished, so had the girls.

Queen and King Wiseheart grieved day and night. Every day felt like winter. In time, though, the queen gave birth to another child, a son they called Ivan. The king and queen were wiser than before, and this time they built no more walls around the castle.

Ivan delighted everyone with his wit and kindness, but his greatest joy was to play the harp. Ivan played so well that when people heard his music, they forgot their cares and began to dance, arms akimbo, whether they wanted to or not.

One day, the king told Ivan, "My son, you are good, strong, kind, and wise, and I am pleased with you, except for one thing. When I am gone, how will you defend our land? You lack the skills of a warrior."

"Trust me, Father. Try me today. Call your soldiers together, and if one of them offers to rescue my sisters from the whirlwind that carried them away, I'll wash his pots and pans for a year."

So the king called his soldiers together and asked. The men hid behind each other and no one offered to go. Who knew how fight a whirlwind?

Ivan stepped forward. "I'll go, Father."

"Then take all the soldiers, horses, and spears you need."

"All I need, Father, is my harp and my wits. Give me a year and a day to be gone and back."

So Ivan went on his way, high and low, near and far, always playing on his harp. At night he slept beneath the stars, and at dawn he traveled onward. One evening, he came to a clearing in the forest where a little hut twirled about on long red chicken legs. Though he was frightened, Ivan called out,

Turn 'round, little house, turn 'round. Let your door be found.
Let your door open wide. I want to come inside.

At that, the little hut stood still and the door opened. Ivan entered a small room hung about with herbs and flowers. There sat Baba Yaga, the bony witch of the woods. "Fie! Fie! Fie! How dare you

come here, where no Russian soul dares enter?"

Ivan yawned. "Ask me no questions tonight, little granny. Morning is wiser than evening. Right now, I need food and sleep."

Ivan's fearless answer so surprised Baba Yaga that she leapt up, cooked a turnip stew, and made a soft bed for Ivan. In the morning, Ivan asked Baba Yaga if she knew where his sisters were.

Shaking a finger of warning, she nodded, "They're prisoners of a nasty fellow, the Little Man No Bigger than Your Thumb with Mustaches Seven Miles Long. A fierce little fellow, he is. He can uproot oak trees with his bare hands!"

"Even if he is ten times stronger than any man, he will not keep my sisters!" said Ivan. "Where does he live?"

"The way to his cave is long and difficult, but not far from here is a farmer's cottage that he carried off last week. If you catch him there, you'll be saved a dreadful journey."

Ivan thanked Baba Yaga and set off. When he came to the cottage, he knocked at the door but got no answer, so he went in and sat down. But the little man didn't come and didn't come, so Ivan went to the garden, picked the biggest cabbage he could find, and began to cook cabbage soup.

At once, there was a thundering and rumbling. Down from the sky in a whirling cloud of shadow and light came the Little Man No Bigger than Your Thumb with Mustaches Seven Miles Long. "HOW DARE YOU COME INTO MY COTTAGE AND COOK MY CABBAGE!" he shrieked.

"You ought to grow a little bigger before you shriek so," said Ivan.

With that, the Little Man seized the doorposts and shook the whole cottage until it creaked. So Ivan grabbed both ends of the Little Man's mustaches and began to swing him about in the air. Writhing like a serpent and with a terrible wrench, the Little Man pulled loose, leaving only the tips of his mustaches in Ivan's fists, and vanished in a whirling cloud of shadow and light.

Then Ivan went to a nearby river and began to ferry people across, asking every passenger where the Little Man might live, but no one could say. One day, three old men offered to pay him for the crossing in gold and pearls.

"I want neither gold nor pearls," said Ivan.

"Ask whatever wish you wish, then," they said.

"Let me be where the Little Man holds my sisters!" And before he could blink, Ivan found himself on a rocky shore below a gloomy cave where the Little Man No Bigger than Your Thumb with Mustaches Seven Miles Long stood guard.

"I've come for my sisters!" called Ivan.

The Little Man rushed into the cave and dragged out the two girls by the arms. "LEAVE HERE AT ONCE OR I'LL HEAVE YOUR SISTERS ONTO THE ROCKS!"

Ivan grabbed his harp and began to play a lively tune. Instantly, though he did not want to, the Little Man let go of the girls, set his arms akimbo, and danced, and he could not stop dancing. Ivan set down the harp and bid it to keep on playing, so the harp went on harping without a harper.

Loveliness that Shines and Jewel without a Price ran into their brother Ivan's arms. Hand in hand, the three of them fled that rocky shore.

As the harp kept harping, Little Man kept dancing, arms akimbo. At the sound of the harp, fish came out of the sea, and whales and sharks, lobsters and crabs, dolphins and eels, and they all danced around the Little Man and could not stop dancing. For all we know, the harp may still be harping without a harper somewhere on the shore of Russia beside the ice-blue sea.

To celebrate the return of their three children, Queen and King Wiseheart tore down the walls around the castle and invited the whole kingdom in for a feast.

18. MOLLIE WHUPPIE AND THE BIG, BAD GIANT (Wales)

Once upon a time, a family of woodcutters had so many children that they could not feed them all, so they sent the three oldest, all girls, out into the world to find their own way. The three girls wandered and wandered through the woods until they came to a gloomy stone house, where they knocked upon the door.

A frightened-looking woman peeked out. "What do you want, girls? What do you want?"

"We're all alone in the world, and we're cold and tired and hungry. Please, can we have a bite of bread and a cup of milk?"

"Well, come in then, but be quick, as my man's a giant, and if he comes home and sees you, watch out."

No sooner had the girls taken a bite of bread and a sip of milk than in at the door came the giant. "FEE FI FO FUM! WHO HAVE YOU THERE, WIFE?"

"Just three traveling girls, and don't harm them! They're all alone and have no home."

"WELL, THEN, LET'S HAVE THEM SPEND THE NIGHT!"

That night, the giant sent the three traveling girls and his own three daughters up to sleep in the same big bed. But before they went, he put ropes of gold around his own daughters' necks and ropes of straw around the three traveling girls' necks.

While the others fell asleep, the youngest traveling girl stayed awake. Her name was Mollie Whuppie, and she was very clever. She switched the ropes of straw with the ropes of gold so that the giant's daughters wore the ropes of straw while Mollie and her sisters wore the ropes of gold. Then she sat back in the dark to wait.

Sure enough, in the middle of the night, in came the giant. He felt around in the bed for the ropes of straw and pulled those three girls out, lifted a trapdoor in the floor, and down they went. Then the giant went off to bed.

Mollie woke her sisters and they ran and ran and ran until they came to a castle. They went in, and Mollie told the king their story.

"Well, well, Mollie Whuppie," said the king. "You've managed finely, but if you would manage even better, go back and bring me my sword, which the giant keeps over his bed. If you can do that, I'll give your oldest sister my oldest son to marry, if she and he agree." Now, this king had three of the handsomest, kindest sons that Mollie and her sisters had ever dreamed of, so Mollie said, "I'll try!"

Back she went through the woods to the giant's house and hid under his bed. Home came the giant. He ate his dinner in one big bite and fell into bed with a giant snore.

Mollie reached up and began to lift the sword from the hooks above the bed, but just as she got it to the edge of the bed, the sword gave a rattle and the giant woke up. And she ran and he ran and she ran and he ran until they came to the Bridge of the One Hair. Mollie got over, but the giant, being too heavy, couldn't.

"WOE TO YOU, MOLLIE WHUPPIE! NEVER COME AGAIN!"

"I might, and I might not," said she. Back she ran to the king and gave him his sword, and Mollie's oldest sister married the oldest son that very day.

"Well, well, Mollie Whuppie," said the king. "You've managed finely, but if you would manage even better, get my bag of gold that giant keeps beneath his pillow. If you can do that, I'll give your middle sister my middle son to marry, if she and he agree."

Mollie said, "I'll try!" and back she went through the woods to the giant's house and hid under his bed. Home came the giant. He ate his dinner in one big bite and fell into bed with a giant snore. Mollie reached up and began to pull the bag of gold from under the pillow, but just as she got it to the edge of the bed, the coins gave a rattle and the giant woke up.

Then she ran and he ran and she ran and he ran until they came to the Bridge of the One Hair, and she got over but he couldn't.

"WOE TO YOU, MOLLIE WHUPPIE! NEVER COME AGAIN!"

"I might, and I might not," said she. Back she ran to the king and gave him his bag of gold, and Mollie's middle sister married his middle son that very day.

"Well, well, Mollie Whuppie," said the king. "You've managed finely, but if you would manage even better, go get my ring that the giant wears on his finger. If you can do that, I'll give my youngest son to you, if you and he agree."

Mollie said, "I'll try!" Back she ran through the woods to the giant's house and hid under his bed. Home came the giant. He ate his dinner in one big bite and fell into bed with a giant snore. Mollie began to pull the ring from his finger, but just as she got it to the tip the giant woke up and grabbed her.

"WELL, WELL, WELL, MOLLIE WHUPPIE! IF I HAD DONE AS MUCH ILL TO YOU AS YOU HAVE DONE TO ME, WHAT WOULD YOU DO TO ME?"

Mollie thought. "I'd put you in a big sack and hang the sack on the wall and go into the woods to get the biggest stick I could find, and I'd come back and hit you with it!"

"HA HA HA! MOLLIE WHUPPIE, THAT'S JUST WHAT I'LL DO TO YOU!" The giant put Mollie in a sack and hung the sack on the wall and then went out to get the biggest stick he could find.

All Mollie did was say, "Oh, if only you could see what I see!"

The giant's wife said, "What do you see up there, Mollie? What do you see?"

"Let me down and I'll tell you," said Mollie.

So the giant's wife let Mollie down, and Mollie said, "I can see you and your daughters living in a sunny cottage far away from this gloomy place."

"Oh, Mollie, I can see that too!" The giant's wife called her daughters and they all ran away to a happier life.

Then Mollie put a rock and a bag of flour in the sack, hung the sack back on the wall, and hid behind the door.

In came the giant with the biggest stick he could find and he pounded on the sack. The sack broke open, the flour flew out, and the rock fell onto the giant's foot. He howled and sneezed and howled and sneezed. Then he saw Molly run out the door. Then he ran and she ran and he ran and she ran until they came to the Bridge of the One Hair, and Mollie got over but he couldn't.

"WOE TO YOU, MOLLIE WHUPPIE! NEVER YOU COME AGAIN!" said he.

"I might not!" said she. And Mollie never did see that giant again. Back she ran to the king, and gave him his ring.

"Now you may have my youngest son for yourself," said the king.

"He's lovely," said Mollie, "but first I want to see the world."

"May I come, too?" asked the prince. And away they went.

19. WILD ONIONS

(Central California)

One spring afternoon when the rains had stopped, six Mono women (whose husbands were away hunting) and a little girl went up a mountainside to gather clover. One of the women discovered a new food, wild onion—a small bulb with starry white flowers and a crunchy, tangy taste. Delicious! All the women agreed that they had never tasted anything so good. They ate wild onions all afternoon and carried home bunches of them.

That night, their men returned to the village, hungry from hunting. But when they entered their homes, the men sniffed and said, "Phew! What's that smell?"

"A new food we found: wild onions! We'll show you where they grow. Try one."

"No, thank you! Your breath smells bad enough. Please sleep outside tonight."

The women smelled so strongly of onions that even their mothers wouldn't let them sleep in their houses. For the first time ever, the six women and the little girl slept out under the stars.

But the next day, no sooner had the men gone hunting than the women and the little girl hurried right back up the mountain and ate wild onions all afternoon.

That night, when the men returned from hunting, none of them had caught anything. This had never happened before. "The animals must have smelled that awful smell on us and run away." When the men caught the scent of onions on the women's breath again, they yelled, "Now you smell worse! Stay out of our houses and sleep outside!"

Again, even the women's mothers would not let them sleep in their houses. And so once more, the six women and the little girl slept outside together under the stars.

On the third day, with the onion smell getting worse and worse, the men had a fit. "Go away! Go away! We can't hunt. We can't sleep. We can't stand it. We will get new wives—women who will stay home."

"If our men no longer want us, we should leave forever," said one woman. They had actually begun to enjoy their adventures together and sleeping under the stars. In the morning when the men woke up, the six women and the little girl were gone. Each had taken her own magic rope of eagle-down and hiked up to where the wild onions grew.

"Now it's time to use our magic," said the leader of the women. She said an old and powerful magic word and then threw her eagle-down rope up into the sky. One end of the rope caught onto a cloud, while the other end trailed back down to earth. Then each woman and the little girl tied her own eagle-down rope to the end of the leader's rope. Standing on the ends of their ropes that lay on the ground, the women and the little girl held hands in a circle and began to sing an old and powerful magic song. As they sang, the ropes began to rise and spin, rise and spin, rise and spin. Soon the women and the girl were twirling in a great circle over the village.

When their mothers saw their daughters rising in the sky, they cried out, "Come back! Come back!" They brought out beads and blankets and food from their houses and held them up as gifts, begging the women to return.

But the women and the girl kept singing and spinning upward.

When the six husbands saw their wives rising in the sky, their hearts ached with longing. They grabbed their own magic eagle-down ropes, and then their leader said the men's own old and powerful magic word and threw his eagle-down rope into the sky. One end caught onto a cloud, and the other end trailed back down to Earth. Each man tied his rope onto the end of the leader's rope. The men sang their own old and powerful magic song and then they too rose up into the sky. Singing and rising, singing and rising, they went twirling after the women.

But the women's circle had started earlier, so they were already higher than the men. In time, the women, the little girl, and the men all turned into stars. Every spring, a constellation of six bright stars plus one smaller star returns to the sky of the Northern Hemisphere, where it stays for the rest of the summer. Some cultures call it the Seven Sisters, or the Pleiades, and some know the grouping as the stars that make up the face of the constellation Taurus, the bull. Just below these seven stars is another grouping of six stars; the Mono people call these two constellations the Young Women and the Young Men. On clear nights from late spring to late summer, you can see these two circles of tiny white stars twinkling in the sky above, close together and shining with the brightness of love.

And just think, it's all because of wild onions.

20. THE GIRL WHO SAID NO!
(Norway)

Once there was a rich squire who had bags of money, lots of land, and a grand house with many servants. One thing he didn't have was a wife, but he was sure that he could easily get one. What girl wouldn't want to marry a rich squire?

As he rode around looking, the squire saw a girl with thick blond braids, pink cheeks, and strong arms working on her father's small farm nearby. Right away, he liked the look of the girl and wanted to marry her.

From up on his horse, the squire looked down at the girl. "Young lady, I want to marry you." He was sure she would say yes right away, but she didn't.

She looked up at him, shook her head, and said, "No, sir, no, thank you."

"But I have a grand house and many servants. You would never need to work again."

"Thank you, sir, but my answer is no!"

"But I have bags of money in the bank and lots of land."

"Please, sir, I have said no twice. Thank you, but I don't want to marry you."

The squire went straight to the girl's father. "I will give you lots of land and bags of money if your daughter will agree to marry me."

The girl's father liked the offer very much. "I will speak with my daughter and I will get her to marry you, I promise."

But no matter what her father said, the girl refused. "Even if he were the richest man in the world, I do not want to marry him. He did not ask what I want, and he does not even care. So I do not love him even one tiny little bit."

After three weeks of waiting, the squire sent for the girl's father. "You promised me your daughter. We agreed on the terms. So where is she?"

"Well, since my daughter will not obey me, you must get her another way. Prepare everything for the wedding and then call for my daughter. Tell her you need her to help with the harvest."

"And then what?"

"As soon as she arrives, dress her in a wedding dress and say the wedding vows right away before she can say no. Once she is married to such a fine squire with a grand house, she'll like being your wife, I'm sure."

The rich squire thought that this was a clever plan. The next day, invitations were delivered to the neighbors. A seamstress sewed the wedding dress. The squire's cook prepared a wedding feast and baked a wedding cake. Then the squire's coachman drove off to fetch the minister.

Finally, they needed the bride. The squire called to a stable boy, "Hurry to my neighbor's house and tell him to send over what he promised me, right now. "

The stable boy ran to the girl's father's house. "My master wants what you promised him. He's waiting."

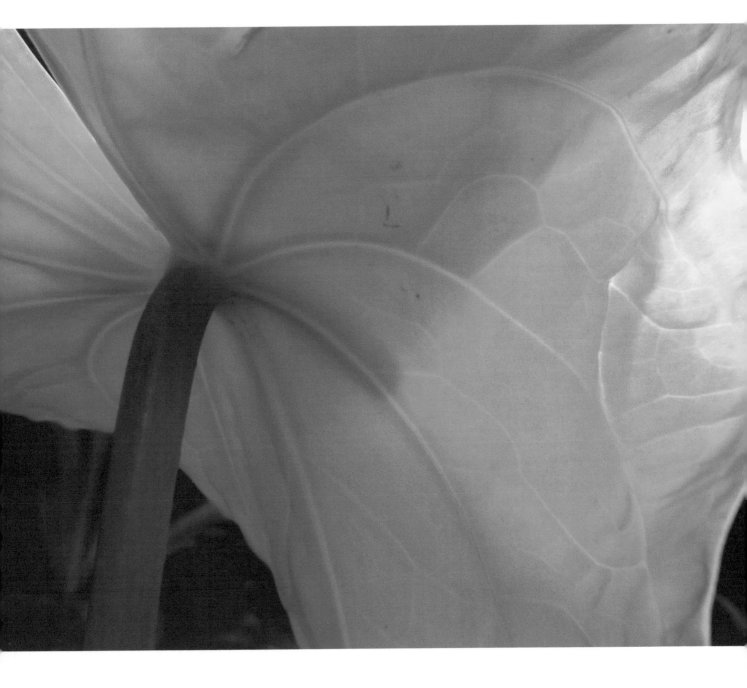

The girl's father pointed to the meadow. "There she is, out in the field. Just run over and take her to your master."

The boy ran out to the meadow where the farmer's daughter was working. "Good morning, miss. I've come to get what your father promised to my master."

The quick-thinking girl guessed what the men were planning. "Oh, yes, there she is, over by the fence, the little bay mare that my father promised to your master."

The boy thanked the girl, jumped on the little bay mare, and galloped back to the squire's house. "She's here, sir, right outside."

"Well, hurry up and bring her in and take her upstairs."

"Upstairs, master? Up the stairs?"

"And hurry up, you lazy bones!"

"I'm not so sure I can get her to go."

"What is wrong with you, boy? Just do as I say and be quick."

When the boy came back downstairs, he groaned. "That was the hardest job I've ever had to do, sir."

"Stop your grumbling and send the women up to dress her," said the squire.

"Dress her, master? Dress her?"

"Get moving, you nitwit. Right now!"

So the boy sent the women upstairs. After a struggle, they got the dress and the veil on the little bay mare. The boy called down, "She is ready, sir."

"Come right down with her then. All the guests are waiting and the minister, too."

With the women and the boy helping, the little bay mare came clomping and tromping down the stairs.

When the squire saw the little mare dressed as a bride, he threw up his hands and covered his face. "Oh no!"

When the wedding guests saw the little bay mare coming down the stairs dressed as a bride, they all began to laugh, and they could not stop laughing. Even the minister had to laugh.

The little bay mare ran out the front door, tattering her wedding dress to shreds, and galloped all the way home.

The squire went up to his room and did not come out at all that night. Never again did he try to trick a girl into marrying him.

21. THE WOMAN WHOSE EYES COULD FLY (Hawaiʻi)

Long ago in Hawaii, Keawe and his wife Anahaki lived happily on the island of Oahu. Every day, Keawe went to the mountains to pick fruit and gather wood. Then he went out to sea to catch fish. His days were so busy that he had little time to spend with his six children.

One day, Anahaki said, "After you return from the mountains, I will go and fish for us so that you have time with the children." Keawe agreed, so after he returned from the mountains, Anahaki went down to the sea.

Now, Anahaki had strange and wonderful powers that she had always kept secret, even from Keawe. When she reached the seashore, Anahaki went to a cove hidden from the sight of the other fishermen. There she chanted,

> *O right eye, fly out and bring me fish!*
> *O left eye, fly out and bring me fish!*

Both her eyes fluttered out over the sea. When Anahki called them to return, her right eye fluttered back, bringing fish, and her left eye fluttered back bringing fish. Anahaki divided all the fish into eight portions for her husband, their six children, and herself, and they had a fine dinner.

But the next day, after using her strange and wondrous powers all afternoon, Anahaki felt tired and hungry, so she ate one fish after another, until only a few fish remained.

That night, when Keawe saw how much smaller her catch was, he looked disappointed. "Anahaki, what happened? Was this the best you could do?"

The next day, Anahaki again returned with only a few fish. And the next day, too. Finally, Keawe grew suspicious. How could Anahaki have such good luck one day and such bad luck afterward?

A wise old woman in the village whispered to Keawe, "Anahaki has strange and wondrous powers to send her eyes out to catch fish." She told Keawe how to catch Anahaki. "Gather leaves from the *ipu'awa'awa* plant, then follow your wife to the shore. When she calls back her eyes, catch them with those leaves in your hands."

So the next day, when Anahaki left to go fishing, Keawe snuck out and followed her.

When Anahaki reached the shore, she chanted,

O right eye, fly out and bring me fish!
O left eye, fly out and bring me fish!

Out fluttered both her eyes, and they caught many fish.

Keawe walked up silently behind his wife, who could not see him, for without her eyes she was blind. When Anahaki called for her eyes to return, Keawe caught them both in the *ipu'awa'awa* leaves and wrapped them up. He then gathered up all the fish that Anahki had caught and went home.

Anahaki stayed on the shore calling for her eyes, calling and calling, wondering why her eyes did not come.

When Keawe reached home, his hungry children gathered around the fish. Five of the children were too busy eating to notice, but the sixth child, a little girl, saw Keawe hide a small bundle on a high ledge.

Meanwhile, Anahaki waited on the beach, still calling and calling, but her eyes did not come back. Finally, stumbling and groping, she found her way from the shore back to their hut. When she asked the children if their father had returned, they said that he had, and he brought many fish. Anahaki asked if he had come back with something smaller too.

Five of the children said they had seen nothing, but the smallest one, the little girl, told her mother that she had seen Keawe bring home a small bundle wrapped in *ipa'awa'awa* leaves. She led her mother to where the bundle was hidden. Anahaki unwrapped the bundle and put her eyes back in.

When she saw her children looking so happy and well fed, and the look of love and understanding in Keawe's eyes, she forever after always brought home all the fish that she caught. And she also always brought an extra fish for the wise old woman who had whispered her secret to Keawe.

22. THE GIANT WITCH BABY WITH IRON TEETH (Russia)

Once there was a little boy called Ivan, who, from the day he was born, never said a word. His parents, the king and queen, felt sure that he would never make a good ruler, so they took no care of Ivan. Every day they wished for another child. And for that wish they were sorely punished, as you shall hear.

Little Ivan spent all his time at the stables with a wise old groom who knew the past and the future and what goes on underground, which he had learned from the horses.

One day, the old groom said, "Little Ivan, tonight you will have a little sister, and a bad one, for she's a witch with iron teeth. She will grow like a seed of corn. In six weeks' time, she will be full-grown. With her iron teeth, she will eat your father and eat your mother, and eat you too, if she gets a chance, so you must escape. Ask your father for the best horse in the stable and then gallop away like the wind to the end of the world."

So little Ivan ran to his father, who held a baby girl in his arms. She was screaming in fury. "What a voice this one has," said his father proudly.

"Father, may I have the best horse in the stable?" asked Ivan.

"Finally you can talk? Yes, take the horse and go. Look what a fine little girl your sister is! She already has all her teeth. It's a pity they are black, but that might change."

Little Ivan shivered, for he knew her teeth were iron. He thanked his father, ran to the stable, and jumped onto a great black stallion. He waved goodbye to the old groom and galloped off to find his way to the end of the world.

He leapt rivers and streams and passed people and houses, until he began to feel lonely.

Suddenly, on a vast, empty plain, he came upon three old women sitting in the middle of the road and bent over their sewing. When one broke a needle, they all helped to thread a new one and went on sewing.

In a cloud of dust, Ivan pulled up.

"Good day, grannies. If this is the end of the world, let me stay and live with you so I can be safe from my baby sister who is a witch with iron teeth and grows like a seed of corn. I'll gladly thread your needles for you."

"Little Ivan, this is not the end of the world. It will do you no good to stay here, for as soon as our last needle is broken, we shall die and your baby sister would have you and eat you in a minute."

Little Ivan cried, for he was little and all alone. But off he rode on the great black stallion toward the end of the world.

Then, in a great oak forest, Ivan came upon a giant named Tree Tosser, who uprooted and tossed down trees to take to market.

"Is this the end of the world? Can I stay here with you and be safe from my baby sister who has iron teeth and grows like a seed of corn?"

"This is not the end of the world, and you would not be safe here," said Tree Tosser. "For as soon as I toss down the last tree, I will die and your baby sister would have you and eat you in a minute. And there are not many trees left."

Little Ivan cried, for he was little and all alone. But off he rode on the great black stallion until he came to the mountains. There was a terrible roaring and crashing as whole mountaintops broke apart, flew into the air, and tumbled down. There stood the giant named Mountain Smasher, who was beheading the tall mountains.

This must be the end of the world, thought Ivan. "Please, Sir Giant, may I stay here and live with you and be safe from my baby sister who is a witch with iron teeth and grows like a seed of corn?"

"This is not the end of the world," rumbled Mountain Smasher as he dusted off his huge hands. "And you would not be safe here, for as soon as I smash the last mountain, I shall die and your baby sister would have you and eat you in a minute. And there are not many mountaintops left." The giant turned back to his work, and once more the sky filled with flying rocks.

Little Ivan cried, for he was little and all alone. But off he rode on the great black stallion over the wide world until at last he came to the end of the world. There, hanging in the sky above him in the rosy clouds, was the glowing castle of the Little Sister of the Sun. "I should be safe up there," thought Ivan.

Just then, the Little Sister of the Sun opened her tower window and saw him. She beckoned and called, "Ivan, come and stay here and play with me."

Ivan whispered to his horse, and the great black stallion leapt through the window of the castle in the clouds and landed in the courtyard. Ivan tumbled off the horse and into the arms of the merry Little Sister of the Sun. He laughed because he was so happy.

Every day, the two children played together. When the Little Sister of the Sun grew tired, she let Ivan run this way and that all around the castle in the cloud.

But one day, Ivan climbed to the topmost turret of the castle. From there he could see into the far distance. Beyond the mountains, beyond the forests and the plains, he saw the house where he had been born. The roof was gone and the walls were crumbling.

Ivan wept and wept. His eyes were red when he came down from the turret.

"Why are you crying?" asked the Little Sister of the Sun.

"Because of the wind up there," said Ivan.

But the next day, he climbed again to the turret, and when he came down, again his eyes were red from weeping. Ivan told the Little Sister of the Sun, "I must ride home to see if I can save my parents from my sister, who is a witch with iron teeth."

The Little Sister of the Sun sighed. "Do not leave me, Ivan. I will be so lonely without you."

"I have to find out what happened," said Ivan. "And I will ride back to you as soon as I can."

"But your little sister sounds much more likely to eat you than you are to save your parents."

"Still I must go and see."

"Well, what must be must be. But take these gifts with you." She handed Ivan a magic gold brush, a magic silver comb, and three magic apples. Then she kissed Ivan goodbye.

Ivan rode the great black stallion on toward home. First, he came to Mountain Smasher, who was weeping, for he had no more mountains to behead. "Well, this is the end of me," he mourned.

Ivan threw down the magic gold brush, and up rose a glorious range of mountains tall enough to brush the sky.

"Thank you kindly, little Ivan," boomed Mountain Smasher.

Ivan said, "Now, promise to protect these mountains, and you will live a lot longer."

"I promise," rumbled the giant.

Ivan galloped on across the wide world until he came to Tree Tosser, who was weeping, for he held the two last trees on Earth in his hands. "Now I must die," sobbed the giant, "for there are no more trees left to toss."

Ivan threw down the magic silver comb.

Suddenly, there was a swishing of branches, a spreading of roots, and an unfurling of fresh green leaves, and up rose a great oak forest as far as the eye could see.

"Thank you kindly, little Ivan," said Tree Tosser.

"Promise to protect these trees, and you will live a lot longer."

"I promise," rumbled the giant.

Little Ivan galloped on across the wide world until he came to the three old women who sat weeping in the road. They had just broken their last needle. "Now we must die."

Ivan handed a magic apple to each one. "Here, good grannies, taste these."

With a single bite, the old women became girls again, with raven hair, red lips, and shining eyes. "Thank you, Prince Ivan. Take this handkerchief that we have been sewing all these years. When you need help, throw it on the ground."

Ivan thanked the girls and galloped off toward his old home, which was ruined and riddled with holes. Ivan got off his horse and peeked through one of the holes in the castle wall. There in the great hall sat a giant baby girl sucking her thumb and muttering.

Ate the father, ate the mother, now to eat the little brother.

And then suddenly, as if she sensed Ivan nearby, the giant baby began to shrink and shrink. Soon, a pretty little baby girl ran out of the palace and skipped toward Ivan. "You must be my brother Ivan. Come in and play music for me while I get our supper ready." She handed Ivan a dulcimer and smiled.

Ivan saw her black teeth and shuddered, but he went in to see what he could see and played a tune on the dulcimer while his sister went off to do the cooking.

A little gray mouse poked its head out of a hole. "Give me the dulcimer, Ivan, and I will keep playing. You must run away while you can. Your sister ate your parents long ago. Now she is sharpening her iron teeth to eat you!"

So the mouse played the dulcimer while Ivan galloped away.

When the witch baby found that Ivan was missing, she swelled up in fury, growing bigger and bigger and bigger until what was left of the palace fell to pieces. Then she chased after Ivan.

The great black stallion galloped and galloped, but when Ivan looked back, the giant witch baby, who had swelled up as high as a house, was running after him with long strides, gnashing her iron teeth, going faster than his horse, even though the great black stallion was the fastest horse in the land. When they came to a lake, the great black stallion leapt to the far shore, where Ivan threw down the magic handkerchief. All at once, the lake grew as wide and as deep as an ocean—so far across that the giant witch baby had to swim, and swimming takes longer than running.

She gnashed her iron teeth. "You shan't get away from me!"

Ivan galloped and galloped, but when he looked back, there was the giant witch baby, now thirty feet high, chasing after him and gaining.

When Tree Tosser saw the giant witch baby thundering after Ivan, he threw down a huge pile of trees that the giant witch baby then had to gnaw her way through, and gnawing takes longer than running.

But all too soon, there she was again, thundering after Ivan and screaming, "You shan't get away this time!"

Ivan rode on and on to save his life.

Then Mountain Smasher saw little Ivan with the giant witch baby thundering after him, so he threw down a huge pile of rocks that the giant witch baby had to shove her way through, and shoving takes longer than running.

But soon, there she was again, thundering after Ivan and screaming, "You shan't get away again!"

Just ahead, Ivan could see the glowing castle in the rosy clouds at the end of the world, where the Little Sister of the Sun was waiting at the window and watching for him. Ivan let out a cry of hope.

The Little Sister of the Sun heard, ran to the window, saw the giant witch baby stretching out to grab Ivan, and flung open the window.

The great black stallion leapt through and landed in the courtyard.

Just in time, the Little Sister of the Sun closed and locked the window.

Ivan tumbled off his horse and into her arms.

At that, the giant witch baby gnashed her teeth so hard that they all broke. In a frenzy of rage, she grew bigger and bigger and bigger until she exploded into dust that scattered to the winds.

Now Ivan lives happily with the Little Sister of the Sun in the castle in the rosy clouds at the end of the world. By day, the two children borrow the stars to play with, and at night, they always try to put the stars back in their right places in the sky.

23. THE SPIDER WIFE
(Portugal)

There once lived a boy who daydreamed and sang and wandered about all day. Finally his father and mother decided that their son must learn a useful trade and support himself. The boy had no wish to do so, for he was a happy, carefree lad, but his parents insisted, so he learned the shoemaker's trade. But as soon as the father died, the boy gave up making shoes.

His mother was angry and turned her son out of the house. But the boy promised his mother that he would return home in a year as a rich man. Meanwhile, he said, he planned to marry the first lady he met on his travels. His mother shook her head in disbelief. "Foolish, foolish boy!" she said and shut the door.

The lad left with his shoemaking tools and a loaf of bread in a basket. He journeyed through forests and fields and wild places. One day, he came to a large, square stone, sat down, took out the loaf of bread from the basket, and began to eat. Then, from under the stone, out crawled a pretty little yellow-and-green-striped spider.

As soon as he saw her, the lad said, "How lovely you are! Will you be my wife?" He poked a hole in the loaf of bread, and the pretty spider crawled in.

The lad put the loaf into his basket and walked a great distance, until he came to an old, empty house. He went in and placed the basket on the floor, and the spider crept out. All at once, she crawled up to the ceiling and began to weave a lovely web.

The lad looked up and said, "That's the kind of woman I admire—hardworking and clever."

Then he went to a nearby village seeking work. As there were no shoemakers in that village, the lad was welcomed, and soon he had plenty of work. In time, he was making such a good living that he was able to furnish the old house with a little clay stove, pots and pans, and some dishes. Then he hired a young maid and brought her to the house to help his spider wife.

The spider wife told the maid where she would find everything necessary for cooking and cleaning the house. That night when the shoemaker returned home, he found the house swept clean, and a delicious dinner was waiting. He turned to his spider wife and said, "What a fine choice I made in choosing you!"

In thanks, the spider wife crawled up to the ceiling and threw down some fine embroidered clothes that she had woven for him, plus curtains for the house.

After almost a year of living happily this way, the shoemaker had enough money so that he no longer needed to work at shoemaking. Everything he needed—clothing and food and all else—made its appearance without his knowing exactly how. Feeling rich, he decided to return to his mother's house, as he had promised. He saddled two horses and said to the maid, "Please ride along as my wife, because I am going to tell my mother that I have married, but if she met my real wife, she would say awful things." So the maid mounted one of the horses to go along with him.

Meanwhile, the spider wife had heard everything. She spun down from the rafters, ran outside, crawled up the tail of her husband's horse, and hid behind his saddle.

When they reached the forest, the lad sat down on the same square stone where he had first seen his spider wife. Suddenly, the stone cracked open and a lovely woman with yellow hair and a yellow-and-green-striped gown emerged. The spider wife had become his human wife, and her husband loved her just as much as ever! So he thanked the maid and sent her home.

Imagine the mother's surprise when she met the lovely wife of her foolish, daydreaming son and heard that they lived in a fine old house. And her son was still as happy and carefree as he had been as a boy, and even more so.

24. ANANSI AND THE HAT-SHAKING DANCE (South Africa)

Anansi the Spider hated being the smallest creature at every big gathering. He grumbled, "I'm so small that no one notices me at all!" When Anansi's wife's mother died, he wondered if now might be the time to do something that would make people notice him. Anansi told his wife and their friends Dog, Porcupine, Snake, Rabbit, and Guinea Fowl to go ahead to the mother's village to prepare the funeral feast and that he would come later that day.

Then Anansi sat and wondered what he might do so that everyone would notice him. "I know! To show everyone how sad I am, I won't eat for the whole week."

First, Anansi ate a huge meal. Then he put on his best funeral suit and his best funeral hat and went to his wife's mother's village. All the animals greeted Anansi after his long journey and then led him to the feast.

"Eat, Anansi, eat."

"No, I will not eat. I am far too sad."

So everyone else ate—Dog, Porcupine, Snake, Rabbit, Guinea Fowl, and the rest. All except Anansi.

On the second day when the feast was ready, all the animals said, "Now eat, Anansi, eat."

"No I will not eat. I am far too sad."

On the third day, all the animals said, "Eat, Anansi, eat."

"No, I will not eat."

But on the fourth day, Anansi sat alone in his wife's mother's house, where a pot of beans was cooking over the fire. The beans smelled so delicious that Anansi couldn't wait any longer. He grabbed a spoon and scooped up some beans. Just as he was about to take a big bite, Dog, Porcupine, Snake, Rabbit, and Guinea Fowl came in. To hide the beans, Anansi flipped them into his hat and jammed the hat on his head.

The animals smelled the beans on the stove. "Those beans smell delicious. Now eat, Anansi, eat!"

"No, I will not..."

But the hot beans were burning his head, and Anansi started jiggling his hat.

"What are you doing, Anansi? Why are you shaking your hat like that?"

"I just remembered that back in my old village this was the day of the hat-shaking dance."

"The hat-shaking dance?"

"Yes, yes! The hat-shaking dance. It was the custom in my old village."

At that point, the beans were so hot that Anansi yelped in pain. "OW! Yes, the hat-shaking dance. I must go now...OW! OW!" Jiggling his hat, Anansi ran out of the house.

And all the animals followed.

Even though everyone was watching, the pain was too much and Anansi tore off his hat. Hot beans were stuck all over his head.

When Dog, Porcupine, Snake, Rabbit, and Guinea Fowl saw, they all began to laugh.

Anansi leapt into the tall grass to hide. When he finally crawled out, his friends cheered. They were happy to see him just as he was, and Anansi didn't feel so small after all.

25. THE QUEEN BEE

(Germany)

Once upon a time, two young men went into the world to seek their fortunes, but soon they began drinking and gambling and lost all their money, and they were too ashamed to return home.

Their little brother, a sweet boy, went out and found them. The older brothers only laughed to think that their younger brother could help them succeed, when they themselves had failed so badly. But after talking, the three brothers agreed to travel together.

One day, they came to an anthill. The two older brothers wanted to kick it down and see the frightened ants run about trying to save their eggs. But the youngest brother said, "Let the poor things alone. They are happy, so why bother them?"

On they went, until they came to a lake where two ducks were swimming. The older brothers wanted to catch the ducks and roast them, but their little brother said, "Let the poor things live. They are happy, why kill them?"

Then they came to a beehive up in a tree with honey spilling down the trunk. The older brothers wanted to set fire to the tree and kill the bees to get their honey. But the little brother said, "Let the bees alone. They are happy, why burn them?"

At last, the three brothers came to a castle. A crowd of young men stood outside, but all of them were made of marble. The three brothers went inside the castle and looked around. Soon they came to a door with three locks and a wicket—a small screened window. Through the wicket, they saw an old gray man sitting at a table. They called to him once, then twice, and, on the third time, he rose but said nothing. He came out and led the three of them to a table covered with delicious food. Afterward, the old man showed them to their rooms.

In the morning, the gray man woke the oldest brother and showed him three tablets. Written on each one was a task needed to break a spell that had been put on the castle. The first tablet said: "In the woods and under the moss lie the thousand pearls of the king's daughters. Find every pearl or be turned to marble."

So the oldest brother went to the woods and searched the whole day, but when evening came and he had only found the first hundred pearls, he was turned to marble. The next day, the second brother tried, but he succeeded no better, for he found only the second hundred pearls, and he too was turned to marble.

At last, the little brother took his turn looking in the moss; but it was so hard to find all the pearls that he sat down upon a stone and cried. As he sat there, an ant from the anthill he had saved came to help him and brought five thousand more ants. Soon the ants found all the pearls and laid them in a heap, so the young brother was saved.

The next day, the gray man showed the little brother the second stone tablet, which said: "Fish the key to the girls' bedroom from out of the lake." When the little brother went to the lake, he saw the two ducks whose lives he had saved. At once, the ducks dove to the bottom and brought up the key. So for a second time, the youngest brother was saved.

Then he faced the third task, which was to choose the wisest of the king's three daughters. Three lovely girls appeared, and they all looked exactly alike. The gray man told the boy that one girl had eaten a spoonful of sugar, the next one a spoonful of maple syrup, and the third one a spoonful of honey, and the boy had to guess which one was the wisest. The boy went from girl to girl, not knowing how to choose, and finally he cried in fear for his life.

Then a bee flew in—the queen bee from the hive he had saved. She hovered over the lips of each girl and then stopped on the lips of the one who had eaten the honey, for honey stays sweet, lasts the longest, and is the healthiest sweetener. The little brother knew then that she was the wisest, so he chose the daughter with honey on her lips. He was saved a third time, and so broke the spell on the castle.

The two brothers and the other young men who had been turned to marble woke up and went home, older and wiser. But the little brother stayed on with the king's daughter and their love lasted and stayed as sweet as honey.

ACKNOWLEDGMENTS

My gratitude goes out to so many who helped to light my way.

Thanks to my beloved children, Amanda and Cannon, who listened first.

To my grandchildren, Gus, Jane, Nick, Luke, and Drake, who listened, too. And to children everywhere who listen still.

With gratitude for the kindness of Justine and Michael Toms of the New Dimensions Radio Foundation, who asked Joseph Campbell to mentor my first recording, *Children of Desire: Five Creation Stories from Around the World*.

To Malcolm Margolin, who introduced me to Darryl Babe Wilson, who shared his Achomawi stories from the Mount Shasta area.

To Rosemary Verey, who published my essay "A Child's Inheritance" in her book *Secret Gardens*.

To Charles Reich, who mapped the entwined lineages of democracy and ecology.

To Vicki Noble, who unearths female spiritual traditions worldwide.

To Laura Simms, who lights my path in storytelling.

To Terry Clarke, my sweetheart and partner in tango and travel.

And with special thanks for my production team: Molly Woodward, and Lisa K. Marietta, editors; Ashley Ingram, book designer; and Ted P.Kipping, photographer.

ABOUT BEATRICE BOWLES

Beatrice Bowles performs nationally and internationally in schools and botanical gardens from Filoli Garden in Woodside, CA, San Francisco Botanical Garden, Brooklyn Botanical Garden, and Central Park, NY, and at cultural centers from Spirit Rock in Marin County, CA, Silk Road House in Berkeley, CA, Moonluzza in Portugal, to the Festival of Faiths in Louisville, KY. She is a Fellow of the Garden Conservancy and of the National Tropical Botanical Garden, and a Voting Member of the Grammy's Recording Academy.

Beatrice's five audio storybooks, with original music by Sarah Maclean, are available from Audible.com and at her website (www.beatricebowles.com):

Heaven is a Garden in the Heart

Spark Catchers

Cloudspinner and the Hungry Serpent

The Girl Who Said NO!

The Woman Whose Eyes Could Fly

CPSIA information can be obtained
at www.ICGtesting.com
Printed in the USA
LVHW072145240220
648040LV00021B/787

9 780985 790110